# OPEN FOR MIRACLES

Books in the Valley of Artisans Series
by AmyLu Riley

Remembering

Open for Miracles

A Winter Wedding in the Valley of Artisans

Ordinary Miracles

Join the email list

https://amylu-riley.com/subscribe

# OPEN FOR MIRACLES

## AmyLu Riley

Published by
AmyLu Riley
Evansville, Indiana
United States of America
https://amylu-riley.com

Open for Miracles: Valley of Artisans – Book 2
Copyright © 2021 by AmyLu Riley

Published by AmyLu Riley
Evansville, Indiana, United States of America
books@amylu-riley.com

ISBN: 9781956738025 (paperback)
ISBN: 9781956738032 (ebook)
Library of Congress Control Number: 2021919462

First Edition, 2021

Scripture taken from the New King James Version®. Copyright © 1982 by Thomas Nelson. Used by permission. All rights reserved.

Cover design: Richard Riley
Cover photos: AmyLu Riley, Richard Riley, Tim Bish, Wolfgang Rottmann, Daniel Thomas, Phil Hearing, Peter Muskrat
Author photo: Richard Riley

Typefaces: Sorts Mill Goudy, Libre Franklin SemiBold, Josefin Sans, Lovers Quarrel, Old Standard TT

Printed in the United States of America.

# Acknowledgements

To my husband, Richard Riley, thank you for your love, for always supporting my work, and for making me laugh. I love you.

To my family and friends, thank you for your love, encouragement, and support of my writing. And thank you for helping me by your prayers. I thank God for each of you.

Thanks to Richard Riley for bringing the cover design to life so beautifully. And thanks to Merle Rice and Bea Rice for being enthusiastic first readers of the manuscript.

God, thank you for what you are doing in the lives of readers. You continually astonish me.

## *Chapter* One

WHAT A TREAT it was to have her brother Nick in
town for Thanksgiving, thought River Carter, as
she sipped hot cider and looked around her great-
aunt Della's table at the faces of all those gathered.

Undoubtedly, Uncle Jim—Della's brother and
longtime business partner in the café business—
had hauled out extra table leaves to hold this feast.

River had moved here to the Valley of Artisans
several months ago. But the rest of her immediate
family—River's mother and father, Andrea and
Ted Carter, and her younger brother, Nick, had
converged in the town just for the day.

And, while the family had gathered at Aunt
Della's table for holidays many times over the
years, this was the first time they had been joined
by longtime local painter and gallery owner Sara
Thurston.

Sara was a cheerful woman, friendly and easy to
talk to. It hadn't been a secret that she and Uncle

Jim had been spending time together over the past several months, and everyone was glad to see the pair looking so happy together.

For her part, Sara, with her painter's eye, thought the whole scene made a pretty picture. The table had been set with fall pottery pieces that she recognized as being from River's new line of seasonal tableware: plates, mugs, bowls, a large serving platter, and a soup tureen filled with fragrant pumpkin soup.

River had created several unique fall patterns for her shop and online store, River Carter's Pottery Works, and customer demand for the dishes had kept her busy for weeks.

River remembered that her Grandma Ella used to make miniature pottery pieces to mark various holidays. River had always appreciated the tiny works, but as a potter, she didn't gravitate toward making them. In fact, her work seemed to be getting larger and larger lately. The soup tureen shaped like a pumpkin was enormous. That was alright. Her customers loved them, including Aunt Della, who had been first to snap up a complete tableware set as soon as River had made them.

*Then again*, thought River, *I probably could have fired blobs of unformed clay with glaze poured over them and Aunt Della would have bought them, just to show her support.*

As the assembled group ate, Aunt Della kicked off one of the family's informal traditions.

"I'm thankful to be gathered with so many loved ones," she said simply.

Everyone agreed.

Ted said that he and Andrea were also grateful for all of the good things that had happened for their daughter since River had come to live in the Valley of Artisans earlier that year.

"It's been a packed several months for sure, and I'm grateful for so much," River agreed.

"Which reminds me," she continued, "I also have some news to share. You know how much I loved Grandma Ella's signs and sayings. Well, my friends Kate and Danny—the couple who own the woodworking shop now—and Sara and I started a side venture a few weeks back. We've been making custom signs and selling them online. We called the online store *Signs and Wonders*; we hoped that would be memorable. Anyway, the business has really taken off, to the point that it could probably use its own storefront right here in the Valley."

Sara nodded in agreement, and River noticed Uncle Jim watching Sara with affection.

"Anyway," River continued, *"that's* not something we're even discussing right now. Everyone involved is already too busy with their main businesses to run a second shop. But I just wanted to say that I'm grateful for how well this online side business has gone."

Uncle Jim lifted his mug of hot cider to Sara and River in recognition of this recent positive development, and the others followed his lead.

"Thank you," said River, sincerely. "Okay, enough about me. Nick, what are your plans now?"

Nick said that, having just completed his culinary training, he had begun looking for a job.

"I am finally ready to leave the nest that my parents were probably ready for me to empty long before now," Nick joked, as his parents laughed.

"But seriously, although I know I'll have to start at the bottom in this business, I'm excited to finally be ready to start working in a field I love."

"We're all happy for you, Nick," said Aunt Della. "And I hope you find a job that's just right for you."

Sara was next.

"I am grateful to be here with all of you today," she said. "I'm also thankful that life is getting larger, not smaller, as I get older, and it just seems to be getting more interesting." Here, she gave a warm smile in Jim's direction. "It's wonderful to find that life still has good surprises in store."

"Yes, indeed," said River's dad, Ted, and lifted his tea glass. "Here's to interesting life and good surprises."

River laughed. "I'm happy to wish that for you, Sara—and for all the rest of you, but I'd like my life to stay the same size for a while. It's been plenty interesting this year, and I'm just ready for an even keel." She smiled.

"River, my dear," said Uncle Jim, "while I'm not unsympathetic to your position, I'm afraid that is one hope that is about to be dashed all to pieces by some news Sara and I have."

Jim stood up. With a broad smile at Sara, he announced to the group, "We're getting married!"

Everyone talked at once, and got up from their chairs to hug the happy couple. When they were all seated again, Jim went on to say that there was more, which he had already told his sister Della.

"I'll be semi-retiring from the café, and moving out of my bachelor quarters," Jim said, referring to the guest house behind the café. Jim had worked with Della at the café—and lived in that house— for decades.

"We've decided we'll live at my house once we're married," said Sara.

"Have you set a date?" asked River's mother.

"Yes," Sara replied, looking at Jim. "We've decided on a New Year's Day wedding, and you're all invited."

Everyone talked at once again, not veering at all from the subject until they had eaten their way to dessert.

᠔᠆ᡧ

Accompanied by pumpkin pie and multiple simultaneous conversations around the table, River's brother Nick quietly and tentatively opened a dialogue with his great-aunt about the café.

"I don't want to push in, Aunt Della, but it sounds like there are about to be some big changes here. If you think I could be helpful at the café, I just want you to know I'd be interested in discussing that with you."

Della was surprised. "Nick, what a wonderful idea! But are you sure this place really fits with your ideas for your future? I expected you'd want to start somewhere bigger."

"Aunt Della, this is exactly the kind of place that fits with my ideas. And I would love to work with you and learn from you."

Della was excited at the prospect of another family member coming to live in the Valley of Artisans. Not to mention that her brother's big transition meant she was going to need help—and fast.

Talk at the table had gradually grown quiet as the gravity of Della's and Nick's conversation drew the others in.

"Why don't Della and I take you on a tour of the café after we finish eating, Nick?" Uncle Jim suggested. You've been here plenty over the years, but you probably weren't looking at it as a potential workplace.

"In fact, why don't we include my house?" Jim added. "If you decide you're serious about working at the café, you'll need someplace to live. And the guest house will be empty after January first."

"You'd be welcome to stay with me before then," River offered her brother.

❧

After their coffee cups were emptied, the whole family got up to go on the tour.

"You really didn't think we were going to let you three go alone on this tour, did you?" laughed Sara.

She was already like one of the family, thought River.

As the group moved from the guest house to the café, Sara asked about the stairway at the back of the café's dining area.

"What's up there?"

"It was originally designed to be an overflow dining area," Jim replied, "but at some point, Della put a stop to that."

"I did," said Della good naturedly. "Going up and down those stairs multiple times during meal service was ridiculous. I don't know what we were thinking."

"Is it still set up as a dining room?" asked Sara.

"No, we don't really use it for anything now," said Jim. "Just a storage room."

"We can go up if you like," said Della, waving her hand toward the staircase.

"Oh, this is a nice space," said Sara, as they entered the room at the top of the staircase.

"I don't even remember what's in those," said Della, gesturing to a few boxes along one wall.

"I don't, either," said her brother.

"Apparently everyone is getting along fine without whatever is in them," quipped Ted.

"Because you are my favorite nephew," Della told Ted, "*you* can get away with that."

Ted smiled. He was Della's *only* nephew.

As the group descended the noisy staircase like a herd of stampeding wildebeests to head back into Della's private residence, Sara leaned close to River and remarked, "That upstairs space would be perfect for a sign shop."

❧

When they had nearly restored Della's dining room to order, River's mother said, "Della, I saw the big trunk of evergreen garlands out on the front porch. If you're ready for those to go up, I could help."

Della said that she was, and that anyone who liked was welcome to join them. They all trailed outside. The sun was shining, and, although no one would have said it was warm, it was a good day to be out.

As they worked together on decking the front of the house—and the little white fence—with the long green garlands, strands of white lights, and bold red ribbon, River's mother, Andrea, asked Sara about the plans for the upcoming wedding.

"A friend of mine here in town, Marian Ryan, is restoring an old chapel that her great-grandfather originally built. She's turning it into a wedding chapel," Sara explained.

"Oh, how lovely," said Andrea.

"Is that the one out near the old Davis place?" Ted asked.

"Yes, that's it," said Sara. "Her grand opening is set for New Year's Day, and she wants our wedding to be the first one there."

"That's amazing," said Andrea.

"I agree," said Sara. "Especially since it was really too late to book anywhere, and we had thought it was going to have to be a home wedding. But then this opportunity came up. Plus, Marian is organizing everything, including the photography, which she wants to use in her publicity. It's a great help, since I'll be so busy with WinterFest activities at the gallery."

"I don't think I've ever been to a New Year's Day wedding," said River.

"Did you choose the date to fit in with Marian's plans?" asked River's father.

"Oh, no," said Sara. "We wanted that date. I like the symbolism of a new beginning."

"And I like it because it will make figuring taxes easier next year," said Uncle Jim. Everyone laughed, mostly because they could easily believe it.

In the comfortable quiet that followed, River watched her mother's sturdy hands expertly weave the richly colored ribbons into the garland above the café entrance.

River thought about all the skill in all of the hands represented in this family—and in this Valley. How much beauty came through them for others to enjoy—like the chapel built so long ago that was now going to be put to use again as a place of joyful celebration. River's heart overflowed with a silent petition: *God, let my hands bring beauty into this world for a long time to come through the work you've made me to do.*

Just as an old maxim had predicted, many hands did, in fact, make light work, and soon the café exterior was festooned in green and red, and sparkled with hundreds of white lights.

It was funny, thought River. Decorating the café had seemed just as natural to her family as if they had been decorating their own homes. During Grandma Ella's lifetime, Grandma had hosted plenty of family events at her own home here in the Valley; yet, this café and Aunt Della's house had always felt like the central gathering place for the family. Now, River lived in the house that had been Grandma Ella's, and her family were all still welcome there, but the family orbit still seemed to remain fixed around its longtime center: the café and Della's home.

Della and Jim excused themselves briefly to go inside to fix hot chocolate for everyone and to have a private conversation. When they came out with a tray of steaming mugs, the two siblings had reached some decisions.

River expected that their sequestered conversation had been about Nick, so she was surprised by Aunt Della's next words.

"Jim and I think the time is right to put that space over the café to better use," said her great-aunt.

"That's right," Jim agreed. He then went on to propose an arrangement that would allow the space to be used for the new sign shop, if River was interested.

River didn't know *what* she was. She wondered if her mouth were hanging open. But Sara appeared delighted with the idea.

*She must want it*, thought River. After all, Sara had been the one to mention it on the stairs. *And Jim must think it's a good idea, or he wouldn't have taken it this far. So maybe I should consider it.*

River finally organized her thoughts enough to respond.

"Thank you so much," she said sincerely. "Of course, I'll have to talk to Kate and Danny—and Sara—about it, since we're all in that business together. And figure out how we could staff it. But this is very kind, and I'll give you an answer soon."

Even if they decided not to move forward with the idea, thought River, the kindness *was* a gift.

"And what about you, Nick?" asked Della. "Are you ready to come be my right hand at the café?"

Nick didn't miss a beat.

"Definitely," said Nick. "I would love to."

Nick said he would move to the Valley right away.

Quite a bit of general hugging and back-clapping followed. Aunt Della's eyes were shining.

"Oh, Nick, it will be so great to have you here!" River exclaimed.

"And, River, if it's alright with Aunt Della, I could probably look after the sign shop, too, if it's going to be upstairs here. I could just ring up the sales downstairs at the café counter."

River felt her eyes get wide.

"So much for things remaining the same, my girl," said Uncle Jim, with a kind smile at his great-niece.

## Chapter Two

THE NEXT EVENING, after they all had locked up their respective shops in the Valley, the four business partners of the online sign business— River, Sara, and Kate and Danny—met at the café to discuss the idea of opening a brick-and-mortar sign store in its upstairs room.

As River led Danny and Kate up the staircase from the café dining room to see the proposed space, she tried to take her own temperature on the idea. It felt like a little too much right now. She would be happier if they could all forget about the sign shop and just eat a nice dinner together.

But when Danny and Kate saw the empty room and got a vision for what it could be, they became quite animated. And Sara's enthusiasm for the idea had not flagged.

And then there was the serendipity of Nick's offer to mind the sign store. Of course, they would compensate him for his work, but they wouldn't have to face the immediate expense of hiring.

The whole thing, River could not deny, did seem providential. And it wasn't as if she couldn't use the extra income from expanding their successful online side business; she was sure they all could.

So, why, then, River asked herself, was she being so negative? River told herself that she was looking a gift horse in the mouth, something one ought not do. It was time for her to embrace the idea.

And so, over dinner at the café with her Signs and Wonders business partners, River at last joined in the others' excitement about opening the new brick-and-mortar sign shop, and together they made plans to do just that.

# *Chapter* Three

THE NUMBER OF household items that began to be moved from here to there—and there to here—increased dramatically before the Thanksgiving dinner leftovers had even been eaten.

Nick returned to his parents' house after Thanksgiving just long enough to pack up his belongings. By the end of the weekend, his temporary move to his sister's house was complete. Most of his boxes would sit in River's garage for the next month, awaiting his New Year's Day move to the guest house behind the café.

At the guest house, Jim had already begun sorting and packing. He planned to leave his larger furniture there for Nick to use, except for his desk.

Across town, Sara had begun clearing a room at her house to serve as her new husband's office. Jim would still be doing the books for the café—and he had offered to do the accounting for the sign business, too. He was genuinely happy for Sara and River and their friends to have a good second business, and he didn't want to see River have to spend more time away from the potter's wheel—or Sara away from her paintbrushes—to crunch numbers, when it was something he enjoyed and was happy to help with.

ॐॐ

The next week, however, Sara and Jim turned their attention from the merging of their household goods, to the wedding chapel where they planned to be married in just a few weeks.

Marian Ryan had invited the couple to tour the chapel, even though work was still in progress there, so the three could talk through some planning items related to the ceremony. Marian had said they'd need to come midday—and dress warmly—since there were no lights or heat yet in the chapel.

At lunch time on Monday, Sara slipped away from her gallery and met Jim at the charming old chapel where they would soon say their vows.

Temperatures had plunged unseasonably, and it was so cold in the chapel that their breath hung in the air. Sara was glad they'd been warned to bundle up. How was it possible, she wondered, for it to be more frigid inside a building than outside?

Marian gave the couple a guided tour of what had already been done, and described the transformations that had yet to take place before the chapel's grand opening.

"It will be just lovely," said Marian, seeming to see right through the construction mess and into the future. "And by then we'll have heat, so you and your guests won't have to wear stocking caps and ski pants."

Marian carried her tablet in her right hand, keeping her left hand moving down her checklist. She conversationally peppered the prospective bride and groom with questions relating to their preferences for the ceremony, taking note of each decision, while her facial expressions served as a constant stream of silent compliments on their good taste.

She will do well in this business, thought Jim, whose decades of experience interacting with customers at the café had been a good teacher.

"Do you plan to have attendants?" asked Marian.

"No," said Sara. "This time of year, we didn't want to add to anyone's list."

"Well," Jim said, "beyond asking family and friends to be there on the day."

This, too, Marian received with an approving nod.

As the meeting came to an end, the trio stopped to look down the center aisle. Sara, with her artist's eye for the unseen, could readily envision what a joyful setting this would make for their wedding.

❦

That night, in a much warmer gathering, the Signs and Wonders team met around River's dining table. Danny, Kate, and Sara came to look through some of Grandma Ella's many signs that Nick had brought from his parents' house.

"These won't be sold, of course, but I thought maybe they could help spark ideas," said River. "With a physical store, we're going to need more inventory."

It was exciting to think of their fledgling online sign business growing up and having a place of its own. Their discussion was lively and productive. And when Nick came in later from the café, he joined them, easily falling into the conversation. Everyone was having fun.

But River also noticed another feeling inside. It made her think of walking too fast on a steep downward trail covered with loose gravel and exposed tree roots, and of being unsure of her footing.

She wondered if she was feeling pushed, or if momentum was just naturally building. Either way, it felt a little out of control—unsafe—to her.

She loved Grandma's old signs. And the new ones. Her face relaxed into a smile as she thought of how much Grandma Ella would have loved all of this.

*You can do this,* River told herself, taking a deep breath.

## *Chapter* Four

THE NEXT DAY, River was busy at the wheel in her pottery shop, happily crafting a special winter-themed piece of pottery as a wedding gift for her great-uncle and Sara.

Absorbed in her art, even joyfully humming a meandering tune as she created, River had no way of knowing that not far from where she worked, a scene was about to unfold that could threaten the happiness of those she cared about.

With Nick there now to help Della at the café, and fitting in quite well, Jim was a little freer to come and go as he needed to. Since the weather was good, Jim had decided to move some of the antique pieces of his mother's that he and Sara had decided to keep.

After stowing the items in the garage at Sara's house, Jim thought he would make a surprise visit to his fiancé at her gallery before heading back to the café. But Sara wasn't the only one about to be surprised.

Jim found her at work in her studio at the back of the gallery. Behind a table, head tilted to one side, Sara appeared to be taking in her work with quiet satisfaction. Neither suspected that the peace of that tranquil studio was about to be disrupted.

After greeting Sara and telling her what treasures he'd just moved to her garage, Jim walked around the table to where she was standing and gave her a quick kiss. Then he noticed the freshly-painted sign in front of her. Its hand-lettering read *Open for Miracles*.

"What's that for?" Jim blurted out, dark clouds seeming to gather over his forehead.

"It's an original for one of the new sign patterns we're going to sell at Signs and Wonders."

Jim's mouth formed a hard line. "I'd better get back. I'll see you later on," he said, and made a hasty exit.

Sara wondered what had just happened. Clearly, Jim was upset, but why? Could it be that he thought she had taken on too much, with her involvement in this new side business on top of everything else going on—her gallery business, their wedding, and the combining of their households? That didn't really sound like Jim. Was he concerned that Sara's role in the sign business would somehow take time away from their relationship? That didn't make sense, either; he had been very supportive of the business.

But what *else* could it be?

After closing her gallery that evening, Sara went straight to the café to talk to Jim. It wasn't exactly *anger* she didn't want the sun going down on, but something was definitely not right, and she was determined not to let it fester.

Wanting their conversation to be private, Jim told Della that he and Sara were going upstairs to the new sign shop space for a few minutes.

Nick had already been at work up there in every spare minute, hanging the signs that were already in the online store's inventory.

This was going to look like a real shop, thought Sara.

But although Sara found that progress exciting, there was a far more pressing matter at hand: she needed to know what was on Jim's mind.

She gently asked him, and Jim sighed.

"I think the sign you were painting earlier—the one that says *Open for Miracles*—isn't right," said Jim.

"What do you mean?" she asked quietly.

"I'm surprised you would go along with that," said Jim. "It's misleading."

"Misleading, how?" Sara asked.

"It's just not true," Jim said quietly, concern pulling his eyebrows toward each other. "*Open for Miracles*—that's nothing more than wishful thinking."

"What?" said Sara, stepping backward in surprise and confusion. She tried without success to get her brain around what Jim was saying.

"Jim," said Sara, "I'm glad I came here and asked what was bothering you, because I... I really never would have guessed *that* in a hundred years."

"I just don't think it's right to spread false hope," said Jim. "I wouldn't think you would want to, either."

So, the same message that Sara found encouraging, Jim found upsetting?

"I don't believe it *is* false hope, Jim," said Sara calmly. "I believe it is very true hope."

"Really?" queried Jim with incredulity, peering into her eyes. Now it was Jim's turn to try without success to comprehend how his fiancé could actually believe what she was saying.

"Why—if you feel this way—why didn't you say anything when we named the business *Signs and Wonders*?"

"That's different," said Jim. "I thought you were just being whimsical. And Jesus really *did* do signs and wonders, so they really *did* exist at one point."

Sara's brain darted from one thought to another like the metal sphere in a pinball machine.

Neither of them spoke for what seemed like minutes.

"Well," said Sara, finally, "maybe this is a conversation to continue when we are both well-rested, rather than now, at the end of a long day for both of us. What do you think?"

"Sure, sure," said Jim, feeling as though he were speaking from somewhere millions of miles away, rather than right in front of her. "We can talk about it more later."

The couple walked slowly down the stairs and out to the café porch together, where they said a subdued goodbye in the still, cold air, and Sara left for home in her car.

Jim quietly returned to the warmth of the café, where Della and Nick were busy in the kitchen, talking and laughing loudly as they made pastries to bake for the next morning's breakfast customers. Jim slowly walked through, barely noticing them.

"Oh, is Sara gone already?" said Della.

But her brother didn't seem to hear.

## *Chapter* Five

SHOP OWNERS IN the Valley of Artisans were busy that week, preparing for the start of WinterFest on Friday. This was definitely no time to let their burgeoning tourism business flag, after they'd worked so hard for months to grow it.

Artisans' Guild members had met, brainstormed, discussed, and ultimately agreed on plans for what they hoped would be an enjoyable experience for winter visitors to the Valley. Now, a rapid transformation from the trimmings of fall to the sparkling adornments of winter began appearing all over the Valley.

And so it was that on a Tuesday evening, after closing their respective businesses, River and Kate set out together to a nearby city to shop for seasonal decorations for their stores.

"I'm glad we decided to do this," Kate said. "I can't find any decorations at all in the storage room at the woodworking shop. Maybe Danny's grandpa never decorated it?"

"Well, I know Grandma Ella had some winter decorations she used at the pottery shop, but I sure can't find them," said River.

"They might have gotten stored at the café," Kate suggested.

"Maybe," agreed River. "But with all they have going on, I'm definitely not even going to ask." She smiled.

"Good call," Kate agreed. "So, we're both starting fresh. That reminds me, do you think we should go ahead and get decorations for the new sign store, too?"

"Oh. Yeah," said River, nodding, "we probably should."

"Do you need to get home for dinner with Nick tonight, or should we two eat while we're out?" asked Kate. "Danny's planning to work late in the woodshop, so I'm free."

"No, Nick will be at the café 'til late," River replied, and then laughed. "But, knowing Aunt Della, I don't think my brother will go hungry."

After the two friends had found all the decorations they needed, they chose a soup place they both liked, and sat down at a table.

Kate leaned back and closed her eyes. "This feels like the first chance I've actually had time to relax since... well, I can't even remember."

River laughed.

"Is that the life of an artisan, the life of a shop owner, or both?" River asked.

"Isn't that just life, period?" Kate smiled.

"Maybe," said River, thoughtfully. "But sometimes I wonder."

As the two friends talked, River expressed for the first time some misgivings she was feeling about the sign shop—feelings that she had barely admitted to herself.

"I wonder if I jumped into the whole sign business too fast. Maybe I've taken on too much. I think I may have gotten caught up in the excitement of everything else that happened at Thanksgiving, too—you know, Nick's new life here, and Jim's and Sara's huge announcement. But was this really the right time for *me* to take on more?"

Kate listened, giving River the gift that true friends give best: hearing, understanding, and caring.

❧❦

The next evening, after their stores were closed, Kate and River took turns helping each other decorate the pottery and woodworking shops with their purchases from the night before.

As they place lighted garlands, festive wreaths, and other cheerful touches, they sang along to holiday music from an app on River's phone.

At the woodworking shop, the added noise of Danny's saw joined the music from time to time.

"Danny, I'm sorry you're stuck back there working again while we two play," River shouted over the din.

"Quit distracting me. I'm working with sharp instruments," Danny yelled back, laughing.

"You don't need to feel bad for him for a second," said Kate. "He's practically in heaven when he's woodworking."

"I know the feeling well," said River.

This wasn't the right time to return to the heavier topic of the previous evening, thought River. She just wanted to enjoy the fun of this happy atmosphere with her friend. And so, putting her former concerns out of her mind, River threw herself fully into getting ready for the start of WinterFest.

When the two friends had finished decorating both stores, it was late, so they decided they'd go together the next evening to decorate Signs and Wonders.

ॐ

All was calm and bright the following night when River and Kate arrived at the café. They stuck their heads into the kitchen, where Della and Nick were noisily at work, and greeted the two before heading upstairs to the sign shop with their bags of holiday décor. Jim and Sara were nowhere to be seen—probably busy at their respective homes, River thought, with the work of sorting, packing, and planning how to combine two fully equipped households into one.

Upstairs, as soon as River got her first look at the transformation that had taken place at the brick-and-mortar home of Signs and Wonders, she sucked in her breath.

Nick's labors had come to fruition. He had used every spare minute that week when he wasn't needed at the café to get the sign store ready to open on Friday, in time for WinterFest.

River was amazed at how many signs Nick had gotten displayed in just a few short days. The space no longer looked like a café dining room or a storage room. The shop appeared ready to open. In fact, it *was* ready to open. This was actually going to happen. Tomorrow. It was here. It was real.

The moment should have been idyllic. Instead, an unexpected wave of dread washed over River.

As she and Kate decorated, River tried to force a cheerful expression. But she felt nothing even close to her happiness of the night before, when she and Kate had had so much fun decorating their other shops.

*What is going on?* thought River. *Am I coming down with something?*

Kate seemed to sense River's pensiveness, and worked alongside her friend in good-natured silence. River was grateful.

When they had finished the decorating, the two returned to the kitchen, where River gave her brother a quick hug and thanked him for all of his hard work getting the sign store ready. Then, after goodbyes had been said, River and Kate departed for their respective homes.

## *Chapter* Six

RIVER WASN'T THE only one feeling out of kilter.

Jim and Sara were both surprised at the way their recent disagreement seemed to have enveloped them in a sticky web. Something was definitely different between them now, and it seemed to be bigger than both of them.

As the two continued sorting through their belongings in the evenings, deciding what to keep and what to get rid of, the area of their disagreement weighed on their minds and hearts.

And, although they talked about the matter when they were together, it seemed as if they weren't making much progress.

They each wrestled individually to understand—and, inevitably, to label—what it was, exactly, that they were dealing with.

It wasn't easy, given the fact that each had been unaware until now of the *existence* of the position the other was articulating.

Sara hadn't known that there *were* even believers in Christ who thought that miracles weren't possible. Could she really ever be *one* with someone with such different faith from her own?

And Jim hadn't known there were Christians who *didn't* believe that miracles had ended. What else might he not know about his fiancé?

A question began to creep into Jim's mind: Would he and Sara really be combining households after all?

# *Chapter* Seven

THE ARTISANS' GUILD had ordered red flags to adorn lantern posts throughout the town—flags which had arrived and been put up, exactly according to plan.

The cheerful banners bore bright white lettering proclaiming *Winter in the Valley of Artisans*. Their bold design also featured three white snowflakes per banner—each of the trio unique, of course, as the Guild had specified to the designer—and a silhouette of half of a snowy pine tree at one side.

The banners really were attractive. For many Guild members, it took a conscious effort to avoid pride at the impressive scarlet spectacle lining the streets like a smartly uniformed marching band.

But for one Guild member in particular, pride over the new flags was *not* a temptation. In fact, he grew more bothered every time his eye rested on them. The word *the* on every one of the banners had been treated with a lowercase *t*, and Mr. Lyle, the broom-squire, had serious concerns about whether that was correct. Hadn't his father always capitalized *The* when it preceded *Valley of Artisans*?

And so, at the urging of Mr. Lyle, the Guild, at its next meeting, took up the matter of whether *The* before *Valley of Artisans* should be capitalized in its promotional materials.

Mr. Lyle was allowed to explain his concerns.

"My father always capitalized the *the*," he said. "It just doesn't look right to see it lowercase."

Mrs. Hayes, of the antique mall at the edge of town, who, up until that moment, had not appeared to care whether she were at the meeting or not, and who was not bothered in the slightest measure about the matter under discussion, took the opportunity to weigh in anyway.

"Owners in the Valley are doing this *all different ways*," she said, with a sorrowful shake of her head, "but I think we should be consistent."

River silently wondered how many different ways there could be to capitalize or lowercase a letter.

The other shop owners, eager to get to matters that would affect tourist business and profits, remained impatiently quiet.

Astutely reading the room, Natalie suggested that since WinterFest was already upon them and its promotional materials were already in use, they might table the matter today and take it up at their next meeting for further discussion and a vote. That, she said in a conciliatory manner, would give them time to consider the question and plenty of time to implement an agreed-upon standard in time for their next big tourist event. Someone quickly seconded, and the motion was carried by a vote, to the great relief of nearly all present.

Mr. Lyle appeared perturbed, but silently accepted this thing he could not change.

Mrs. Hayes took a nail file out of her purse and serenely put it to work. She didn't like for these meetings to be a *complete* waste of her time.

# *Chapter* Eight

*I KNOW WHAT the problem is,* thought River suddenly, as she drove home from her Pottery Works late one evening, a few days later.

She had stayed at her wheel several hours past closing time, making more pieces of her winter pottery collection. She hadn't even realized how late it was, she had been so absorbed in her work. Whenever she was at her wheel, time seemed to not even exist for her.

She loved these pieces. As she formed the plates and matching bowls, with their evergreen bough relief along the edges, she could almost smell the soft pine aroma that had enveloped her as she had ridden her bike—before the weather had turned too cold—along a row of evergreens in the Valley, their dropped needles making a rust-colored carpet for her tires.

The collection's mugs, too, delighted her, with their heavy bases, rich glazes, and a generous thumbprint handle that no one—including her—could resist trying for size when they passed by the mugs on the shelf.

River loved every part of the process, from wet clay to final firing.

In addition to larger serving plates and serving bowls in graduated sizes, River had added a matching flowerpot holder to her winter collection, sized to hold a standard poinsettia. She hadn't been sure how well it would be received, but that question had soon been answered by a raft of orders.

Online sales for all of her winter-themed pieces were increasing daily, and River expected that WinterFest in the Valley of Artisans would bring even more buyers to River Carter's Pottery Works. If these winter pieces sold as well as her fall tableware had—and she thought they might sell even *better*—she would have to continue to work steadily to keep up with demand.

*The problem is that I've been working hard, pretty much nonstop ever since I moved here last year, and I just need a break. I probably took a look at that upstairs sign shop and thought, "Here is one more thing that I'll need a break from"—when I already hadn't made time for a break, even before I took on a second business.*

*I just need to plan a vacation. That's what I need: a fun trip to look forward to, to recharge my batteries.*

*And in the meantime, I'll schedule some down time for myself. With all that's been going on, I probably just need a quiet evening to myself.*

River told herself that she would leave work at closing time the very next evening and stay home with a good book. She had a whole stack of them waiting for her. She would brew something hot to drink in a favorite mug, put up her feet, and just read for several hours.

And she would look into some vacation options, too. The way sales had been growing lately, she could afford to make a modest jaunt for a few days to somewhere relaxing. That was it: Right after WinterFest, she would go somewhere *warm.*

She wondered where her hummingbirds were spending the winter. She had read that some ruby throated hummingbirds who spent summers in Indiana migrated as far as the West Indies. She pictured Emerald reclining in a tiny beach chair on the smooth sand, tiny sunglasses resting on his beak. Simon, she thought, probably wasn't the relax-in-a-beach-chair type. He would, more likely, be picking a fight with a coconut.

She'd leave them to it. She didn't need to go *that* far away. But she *would* go away *somewhere* for a few days.

Just thinking about it, River already felt better.

## *Chapter* Nine

RIVER HAD FORGOTTEN, however, that her next evening was already planned. She had previously accepted an invitation from her friend Vera to visit a used bookstore with her in a nearby town.

Over the past few months, the two had discovered they shared a passion for reading. This would be their third visit together to this bookstore. They also planned to stop for dinner on their way back, as they had done on the two previous occasions.

"You know," said River, as she and Vera sat at a restaurant table the next evening, waiting for their food orders, "I was glad to find they had volume two of C.S. Lewis's letters. I had read the first volume and one of his published dairies before."

Vera smiled.

"I shudder to think of my own correspondence being published into volumes," Vera said, after a moment or two. "Can you imagine? *The Complete Texts and Emails of Vera Stanford.*"

River laughed.

"I think that Lewis and his contemporaries must have had *some* idea in advance of their correspondence someday being published," River said. "It seems a little weird, if not."

"Maybe," said Vera, with a tilt of her head and slight raise of one eyebrow as she considered it.

Their thoughts displaced speech for a minute.

"I wonder," River began slowly, "if C.S. Lewis had lived now instead of then, what he might be choosing to publish. I wonder how his work might have been different without those specific gatekeepers who made the decisions that shaped his body of published work. And Tolkien, too. And the rest of them, for that matter. If those writers were alive today, they could truly release anything they wanted. Can you imagine?"

"Do you mean would people still be reading their *mail* a century later?" Vera laughed. "It's an entertaining thought, for sure. I tend to think we're each born in the time we've been specifically created for. So maybe, instead of missing out on something Lewis *could* have written in the circumstances of another era, we have exactly the body of work he was made to create."

"Hm. I wouldn't have thought of that," said River, enjoying herself immensely and feeling very glad she had come out with Vera instead of spending a quiet night at home. She would relax at home with a book tomorrow night, she told herself.

River mentioned nothing to Vera about the sign shop, except to answer her inquiry about whether its new location had opened on schedule.

"It did," said River agreeably, nodding. "We even got it decorated for WinterFest before it opened."

River moved off the topic without further comment, and Vera said no more about it.

# *Chapter* Ten

KATE HAD BEEN baking again.

The woman had a real talent, thought River the next morning, biting into an almond-flour cranberry muffin that her friend had dropped off on her way to the woodworking shop.

River hadn't been the recipient of the cooking genes in her generation—those had mostly gone to Nick. All of them, actually, had gone to Nick. But that was alright with River. She'd rather be making pottery than cooking, anyway. Actually, when she thought of it, she'd rather be making pottery than doing many of the activities that other people seemed to enjoy.

*To each his own,* thought River. *And Kate can share samples of her baking with me any time she wants.*

When Kate came back by the Pottery Works at lunch time to drop off some wooden sign templates Danny had finished sanding, the two friends took a few minutes to chat.

River praised the tasty surprise Kate had brought by that morning.

"I had an ulterior motive," Kate admitted. "After the other night, I wanted to check on you."

"What do you mean?" asked River.

"Well, when we were decorating at Signs and Wonders the other night, it didn't seem like you felt very well or something. I figured you would talk about it if you wanted to, but it's been a couple of days, so I just wanted to make sure you were ok. A while back when we talked, you were wondering if you'd taken on too much. *Have* you? *Are* you okay?"

"Oh, that," said River, nodding. "You are so kind to check on me, thank you. Yes, I did have a moment while we were at Signs and Wonders when I had a really bad feeling about things. But everything is okay now," she said with confidence. "I realized that what I need is to plan a fun vacation."

"A fun vacation?" Kate repeated, as if River had announced that the secret ingredient to a good fruitcake was yellow mustard.

"Yes," said River. "Just as soon as WinterFest is over, I'm going to make some plans for a getaway vacation."

"A getaway vacation," Kate echoed, mentally calculating how many weeks remained before the end of WinterFest.

"Yes," said River. "If I'm going to do everything I want to do, I'm going to need a break every now and then. They say that even just looking forward to a vacation is good for you."

"Do they?" Kate responded.

"Yep, that's the ticket," River replied confidently.

Just then, the bell on the pottery shop door rang as a group of customers walked in, chattering together, surrounded by an invisible mass of cold air. Kate smiled and raised her eyebrows in River's direction, at the positive business development of so many potential customers at one time. Kate moved to go.

"Thank you for checking on me," said River. "I really appreciate it. And thank you again for the muffin earlier. It was great. You've really got a green thumb in the kitchen, or whatever it is that bakers have."

Kate laughed at the image. "You're welcome, and thanks. I'll see you later."

The bell gave another jingle as Kate departed, and River greeted her new customers.

## *Chapter* Eleven

AT THE CAFÉ, Nick continued to work steadily alongside his great-aunt and her brother to learn all he would need to know before Jim's departure.

Nick was a quick study, and he and Della were getting along famously in this new situation. They seemed to share the same sense of humor and regularly made each other laugh, which, under the circumstances, Della found quite a welcome development. She would sorely miss having her brother there every day.

In truth, she was already missing him. Although Jim was fully involved in Nick's training, and was still helping in every way he could at the café, things had already changed.

Change was the main order of business at Sara's house, as well.

When River stopped by there on her way home, as they'd arranged, to give Sara the sign blanks that Kate had dropped off, she was greeted by stacks of cardboard boxes.

"Hello!" called River, as she entered the front hallway of Sara's house. She didn't see Sara, but knew she was expecting her.

One side of the entire length of the hall was lined with cardboard boxes in various states of fullness, succinctly labeled as to the destinies of their contents: *SELL, STORE, DONATE.*

Sara appeared from a back room.

"Where should I put them?" River asked, holding up the armful of wooden pieces.

Sara looked around, finding no empty surface in sight.

"I think I'll just go ahead and put them in my car to take to the gallery," Sara decided.

"I can put them in your car," River offered. "I'll be right back."

When River returned from her short trip to the driveway, Sara was talking on the phone—or, more accurately, listening on the phone. She didn't appear to be receiving good news.

Sara held up an index finger to let River know she'd be just another moment. "Alright, Marian. Thanks for keeping me posted. Goodbye."

"Marian's not sure whether the chapel will be ready in time for the wedding," Sara reported. "I should say *weddings*—she's already got two others in addition to mine and Jim's booked for the first week in January. Anyway, she's been assuring me it's all under control, but now she's having all kinds of unexpected issues with the restoration work—and the wedding is less than a month away."

"Oh, wow, I'm sorry," said River. "What's the matter?"

"You mean what's the matter *today*," said Sara. "It seems like it's been one thing after another— and always some elusive thing I've never heard of before. Now it's some part the electrician needs that's not available, that's holding everything up. But I can't spend too much time thinking about that—it wouldn't do any good, anyway," said Sara, distractedly. "I have my own problems to deal with."

"Problems?" asked River, wondering what Sara meant. In the time River had known the older woman, Sara had always been positive and peaceful. She wasn't the type to focus on the negative, so River found herself surprised at this admission—and, in fact, at this whole conversation.

"Oh," said Sara, faltering a little, "we have too much stuff to fit into my house. Of course, naturally, when you combine two complete households into one, you *would* have more than is needed, and about half of the stuff needs to go. But deciding *which* half, and *where* it's going to go, and then *getting* it there—that's all a time-consuming business. It seems like every waking moment I'm not at the gallery, I'm spending on this."

"Oh, I see," said River carefully, sensing this might just be the tip of an iceberg.

"I don't know why I had to get my heart set on getting married on January first," Sara lamented, "It is such a short timeline for getting ready."

"Mm," River murmured sympathetically.

"I liked the *symbolism* of it," Sara remarked wistfully, as if she were talking about a painting that she had let go and wished she hadn't. "But maybe it would be better...."

Sara began to realize her own thought as she heard it come out of her mouth and quietly let the sentence trail off.

When she saw that River was watching her and waiting for the rest, she simply said softly, "To have more time."

## *Chapter* Twelve

ONE OF THE ideas that had been approved during the WinterFest planning meetings of the Artisans' Guild was to offer horse-drawn carriage rides to visitors during the month of December.

Someone had remembered that one of the local farms used to do this sort of thing, contacts had been made, and the result was that a horsewoman had been found in the Valley who was willing to offer the service, if a plan could be arranged.

On hearing this news, the Bowers, owners of the bed-and-breakfast, had hatched an idea.

Just a few months before, when the couple had decided not to close their business—but to join the effort to build up tourism again in the area—the Bowers had decided to add on to their B&B.

The new addition to their building had been completed on schedule, and all that remained was for them to decorate and furnish it. The Bowers planned to do this time-consuming task themselves—and as soon as possible—in order to make the new space available for paying overnight guests.

But the couple realized there simply wouldn't be enough hours in the day for them to do it all. In order to have the time to commit to the project, something else must give.

They had an idea, but they needed to talk to the owners of the café to learn if it could work.

And so, the Bowers had arranged a meeting with Della and her brother Jim at the café some weeks ago, and a plan had been made: During the month of December, B&B customers would have the option of taking a horse-drawn carriage ride from the B&B to the café to eat their breakfast, compliments of the B&B.

The café would remain closed to the general public on Mondays, as usual, but it would open for a single breakfast seating for the private party arriving from the B&B. Della felt that for just four Monday mornings during the month of December, she could do this to help out the Bowers.

The month-long break from preparing and hosting their guests' breakfast at the B&B would give its owners the time they needed to complete their new addition.

Of course, all of this had been settled before Jim and Sara had made their plans. Della had been concerned about the Mondays after first learning her brother would be leaving. But the fact that the whole arrangement would be concluded before Jim left—and then Nick's arrival coinciding with the start of the plan—had put her mind at rest. And now, thought Della, the extra income she would earn from this short-term arrangement could provide for a nice wedding gift for Jim and Sara.

The arrangement had been put into action as planned at the start of the month, and all involved seemed to be finding it satisfactory—including Debra Reiter, the horsewoman, and the horse, who appeared to greatly enjoy all the attention he received, especially from children.

The carriage business had even begun to grow, as word about it spread and as visitors spotted the majestic horse, followed by its smart driver and smiling passengers, the latter covered by colorful blankets to keep them cozy as they were transported through the Valley of Artisans.

It also hadn't hurt café business to have the beautiful horse and carriage seen sitting out in front each morning, waiting to carry its breakfast party back to the B&B.

࿇

At the next Artisans' Guild meeting, the Bowers were happy to give a report of how the horse and carriage arrangement between the B&B and the café was working out. As usual, Della could not leave her café customers to fend for themselves while she attended a meeting, but she had reported to the Bowers her views on the success of the arrangement, and they conveyed that news to the Guild.

"I think the Bowers are to be congratulated on the idea for this creative arrangement," said Anna, the herbalist.

"I agree," chimed in Alicia, proprietor of the nut shop. "And I hope this venture will continue to be profitable for all of the parties."

Other Guild members also enthusiastically wished the Bowers well, confident that a rising tide lifts all boats.

Natalie, as the Guild's leader, said this was just the sort of experience that tourists to the Valley would remember and tell their friends about.

"If anyone has other ideas like this that they would like to suggest for any season, these are exactly the kinds of things we could all potentially profit from on a continued basis."

Like that moment full of promise when a kite's sail waits only to be filled with a breeze in order to soar, all possibilities seemed open.

And it was that moment that Mr. Lyle chose to speak.

"Getting that *t* done right on our signs is important, and I hope we can get that settled today as you promised."

The metaphorical kite slipped to the ground in a heap.

Natalie thanked Mr. Lyle for his input, and, seeing that this issue had all the hallmarks of the proverbial bad penny that would just keep turning up until she had dealt with it once and for all, asked if there was any more discussion on the matter of the capital or lowercase *the* on promotional signage for the Valley of Artisans, before they brought the question to a vote.

Mr. Lyle peered around the circle at the other businesspeople gathered there, as if his eyes could bore into their thoughts.

Mrs. Hayes said she thought discrepancies in the signage made it look like the right hand didn't know what the left hand was doing.

River silently wondered what discrepancies Mrs. Hayes could be referring to, since all of the new signage was consistent, and, to her knowledge, she had *never* seen any signage in the Valley done the way that Mr. Lyle and his late father were now so insistent on.

River was glad there were no definite articles in *her* new sign. River had ordered a metal sign for the exterior of the pottery shop, featuring the name she had recently decided on for it: *River Carter's*

*Pottery Works.* The sign had been completed and installed just as WinterFest began.

Seeing that no one else was going to speak out in support of his cause, Mr. Lyle changed tactics. "It would be a shame if anything were to happen to the pretty new banners," he began slowly.

Mr. Lyle had *not* understood his audience, nor chosen his moment well. Every member there was impatient to move past this minor point and focus on real issues that would help build their business and profits.

"Vandalism to Guild property over a *lowercase letter?* Who would do such a thing?" said Natalie, pointedly, but not unkindly, in response to Mr. Lyle's thinly veiled threat. "No, I don't think we need to worry about *that.*"

Natalie's gentle but firm tone reminded River of one she had heard mothers of toddlers direct toward their children in the grocery store, when they were coming close to misbehaving.

In the wake of Mr. Lyle's poorly calculated misstep and Natalie's firm response, Mrs. Hayes, who hadn't been sure of how she'd vote on the issue, decided that a lowercase *t* was probably best, all things considered. And so, when it came time to vote about thirty seconds later, only one Guild member preferred the capital *t*.

Kate leaned over and whispered softly to her husband, "Just imagine if all that energy were harnessed for something that mattered." The even-tempered Danny nodded mildly in agreement.

Over a private family dinner that evening in her parents' home, Natalie Bowers wondered aloud if it were possible that any elected leader of the Artisans' Guild had ever faced a less important issue than the one Mr. Lyle had raised.

"Oh, probably," Mr. Bowers replied, good naturedly. "And it probably won't be the last, either."

"Sweetie," said Natalie's mother, "I'm not sticking up for his issue, but Mr. Lyle gave you the key to understanding why that was important to him: It's what he was taught by his father."

"That's why he thinks it's *right*, but why does he believe it's such an urgent matter for the Guild?" Natalie responded. "Why can't he see that it's a microscopic tempest in the very smallest teapot in the world, if even that?"

"Well, now, *that* I don't know," said Mrs. Bowers thoughtfully.

"Some people just *like* tempest, in whatever size teapots they can find," said Mr. Bowers. "Please pass the turnips."

Natalie handed the dish to her father. "Well, I hope we've heard the last of it."

As the evening continued at the Bowers' residence, family conversation turned to more enjoyable topics.

"We'd like to rename the B&B," Mr. Bowers told Natalie.

"Yes, but we're not sure what to call it," Mrs. Bowers interjected. "We thought of having guests submit ideas, or maybe having a contest on our website."

"But we really want to order a new sign for the B&B while we're finishing up the remodel, so we don't want to drag this out," Mr. Bowers concluded.

"If you have any good ideas, we're open to input," said Natalie's mother.

Natalie promised to let them know if she thought of anything.

֍֎

At the café, River and Nick and Aunt Della were having a similar conversation. The café had closed for the evening, Uncle Jim had gone to see Sara, and the three had sat down at a table in the now-empty café dining room to eat a late dinner and to chat.

River had brought some more completed signs from Sara for Nick to hang up in the store, and realized on her way in that the sign shop needed some exterior signage of its own.

"You know," said River to Aunt Della, "while we're getting an exterior sign for Signs and Wonders, we could order a new sign for the café, too, if you want."

"If that means I have to come up with a clever name, I pass," laughed Aunt Della. "Every time Jim and I have tried to come up with an idea other than *café*, we don't get far. I can come up with new recipe ideas all day long, but no name we've ever thought up for this place has stuck."

"Is that why it's always just been called *café*?" Nick asked, seriously.

"Well," said Della, considering the question, "no, I don't think that's always been the reason."

"When our family first came to the Valley of Artisans," said Della, "it was pretty common for businesses here to have simple names. Back then, I guess you could say we weren't focused so much on marketing. When my boys were young and my husband and I ran this place together, I don't remember having to focus on marketing at all.

"I guess the smell of pie just brought people in," she laughed. "We've been blessed that way over the years, in that the locals always recommended this place whenever tourists asked where to eat, and even when tourism business fell off, the locals still ate here."

"Has there ever been any serious competition?" asked Nick.

"No," said Della, "I think the Valley is just large enough to keep us going, but just small enough that no one has ever tried to open another similar business."

"You mentioned that you and Uncle Jim tried to come up with a new name. When was that?" asked River.

"Well, a long time ago, after my husband died, and Jim went into business with me to help run the café, he thought maybe we should come up with a new name for it. But nothing we came up with ever really seemed to fit, so we kind of just dropped the idea. We had plenty else to do to keep this place going."

"You've done an amazing job," said Nick. "Business is steady, the café is profitable, and you're still enjoying your work, even after doing this for decades."

"Thank you, Nick," said Della. "It's true, I am still enjoying it, and it makes me happy to see you here now enjoying it, too. I've always known that my boys' lives were taking them outside the

Valley. But it really was a pleasant surprise when your path led here to the café—especially just as Jim's was taking him away."

"Thanks, Aunt Della," said Nick. "I'm really glad to be here."

"And once again," said River with a smile at both of them, "the café doesn't get renamed."

"You see?" said Della, laughing, "That's a slippery business."

# *Chapter* Thirteen

RIVER RECEIVED NEW shipments of clay and glaze regularly, and sent out online orders daily.

She had gotten into a routine of filling and packing orders first thing in the morning when she arrived at the Pottery Works early, and then tidying and restocking the shelves just before opening. Then she'd open the shop and set to work at her wheel. When customers came in, she greeted them, stopping to ring up sales when they were ready to pay. After a short break to eat lunch, River returned to work. She found that, by keeping to this routine, she was able to both stay caught up with sales and leave work when the shop closed.

River was glad that Nick had taken over the shipping of the online orders for Signs and Wonders. With all of the sign inventory now on display in the room above the café, it made more sense logistically to ship sign orders from there, but that wasn't the only reason River appreciated the arrangement.

Sign sales had continued to increase, and she realized that the additional time she would have been spending on packing and shipping Signs and Wonders orders would have been more than she could have spared from her pottery business this month. *Well, I don't have to worry about that,* she thought, *because Nick is here and he's happy to do it. It's all working out well.*

River tried to take time for herself to relax. On several evenings, as she ate dinner, she picked up a book to read where she had left off the previous night. Many times, however, she found that her mind was too spent from the nonstop day to focus on the page before her.

Sometimes she caught herself daydreaming about summertime. It was too cold now to ride her bike, or to wear sandals, or to do pretty much anything outside except go for a short walk or drive somewhere in her car. And soon, what was left of her flowers—a few valiant pansies making their brave stand against the winter temperatures—would all be under the snow that often came in December. She, along with the bulbs and rhizomes under the dirt, all bore winter patiently, waiting for the signals that a change was coming—one that would lead once again to warmth and color.

What would it be like, she wondered, to live somewhere without dramatic seasonal changes? Even growing up in Tennessee, where her parents still lived, they had had four seasons—though they were milder than the Hoosier winters her dad had grown up with here in the Valley. *I don't mind four seasons,* thought River, *but I'll definitely be ready for a break from the cold, dry winter when it's time for my getaway vacation.*

Some evenings, instead of reading, River flipped open her laptop and explored her travel options. *Where can I go for three days that I won't just want to stay, rather than coming back to the cold?* she wondered. It was a fair question, and one that, so far, she hadn't been able to answer.

One place she did need to go, cold or no, River realized one evening, was shopping for an outfit to wear to the wedding. Nothing in her closet met that need. When she had mentioned the matter to Kate, Kate said she found herself in the same situation. The two friends decided to venture out together one evening to a consignment shop in a nearby city that carried dressy clothing. Kate had heard about the place from a friend, who had found some nice items there.

"I'd like to say my primary reason for wanting to buy from a consignment shop is to go easier on natural resources," said Kate, in the car on the way there, "but I have to admit that once my friend told me about the prices she paid there, I was just as excited about that."

"I'm not judging you," laughed River. "You can have both."

"Like, we can have our clothes, and eat them, too?" Kate said.

River laughed.

"I know we're both doing okay now that our businesses are getting off the ground," said Kate. "But, seriously, we work so hard for every dollar, that it just seems like we should get the most out of them, you know?"

"Well, let me see what they have at this place, and then maybe I'll get up on that soapbox with you," said River.

Inside the store, the two friends fell into the unspoken language of holding up items on hangers for the other's appraisal, followed by nodding, shrugs, or slow head shakes. Quickly enough, they had each gathered a small collection of items to be auditioned in the fitting rooms for the role of Wedding Outfit.

"I wasn't sure at all what I was looking for," said River, "but I think I've found just the right thing." Dressy black pants, a soft, cream turtleneck top with a colorful silk scarf, and a long black sweater should strike a nice balance, River thought, between showing due respect for the happy occasion and not freezing to death. Kate chose a dark suit with a fuzzy sweater in a pretty plum color.

"I hope no one was expecting us to wear dresses," said Kate, as they paid for their selections at the front counter.

"The wedding is in January in Indiana," said River. "If the *bride* wears a dress, I'll consider it an act of heroism."

❧

The bride, in fact, *was* planning to wear a dress, or something like it, but was also going to wear pants. Sara's wardrobe had long been a reflection of her artistic nature, and her wedding attire would be no exception. She had personally hand-painted the silk fabric to be used in the making of her wedding finery, which would be a three-quarter-length dress over loose-fitting long pants.

She had entrusted the precious yards of silk to a local seamstress, who had been at work constructing the garment and was now ready for Sara to try it on.

And so, unbeknownst to River and Kate, Sara was, on the same night they were out shopping for their wedding clothes, trying on her own Wedding Outfit at the seamstress's shop, located in the basement of a sprawling old farmhouse.

"It's perfect," said Sara, looking in the full-length mirror at the way the design she had painted on the fabric worked with the cut and flow of the finished garments to create a graceful sense of movement.

"Good," said the seamstress, pleased at her client's reaction. "You get changed out of that, then, and bring it out, I'll put it in a hanging bag for you to take home."

The seamstress stepped out and closed the door behind her, leaving Sara alone in the room.

Sara made one more slow turn before the mirror, her silk painting moving with her. But she was no longer thinking about the outfit.

She was thinking about miracles, and about what might influence the probability of their occurrence.

## *Chapter* Fourteen

THE NEXT DAY, as River worked at her wheel, she began mentally making a list of the Christmas gifts she planned to give her family and friends. While her pottery seemed like the *obvious* choice, she wondered if it was the best choice in every case.

Nick always had his eye on some new kitchen gadget, so he would probably rather receive some doodad or device for his own kitchen at the guest house.

And since River was already making Jim and Sara a pottery gift for their wedding present, she should probably think of something different for them for Christmas, but she wasn't sure what one got for the couple who already had two of everything, and were trying to get rid of half of it.

And Aunt Della had already bought a complete set of River's winter pottery.

*This is harder than I thought it was going to be,* thought River, *and I haven't even gotten to my parents and Vera and Kate and Danny yet.*

River wondered if there were a way to support local businesses in the Valley with her gift giving. Maybe no one in her family needed a new broom just now, but surely there was something else locally made that they would enjoy?

Clearly, she would need to give this more thought.

River finished the piece she had been working on, and, with practiced hands, removed it from the wheel.

She needed to close the pottery shop during lunch today and make a run over to Sara's gallery to pick up more finished signs to take to Signs and Wonders. Sara had apologized for not having the time to take them herself, but after seeing the state of things at Sara's house earlier, River understood that the bride-to-be already had too much on her to-do list. And since River had already decided that work stopped at closing time, that left the lunch hour.

She decided to make it a real lunch run. She'd phone a food order ahead to Nick at the café and pick up lunch while she was there. First, she called Kate to see if she and Danny wanted something.

"I brought us soup from home," said Kate, "but I sure wouldn't say no to Della's chicken pot pie. We can eat my soup tonight."

River called Nick.

"Nick here."

"Hey, I know you're busy. Can you box up three to-go orders of pot pie for Danny and Kate and me? I'm headed your way to drop off more signs."

"Yep, see you in a few. Watch out for the horse when you get here. He's drawing crowds."

"Thanks, Nick."

The horse, called Major, had become something of a celebrity in the Valley of Artisans and beyond. Video of him pulling a carriage of smiling passengers up the street from the B&B—and then of him patiently standing majestically in front of the café—had been shown on the local news earlier in the month, along with the rather inaccurate caption *Sleigh Ride,* and had subsequently made its way around the internet.

Neither Major, nor Debra Reiter, the horsewoman, seemed to have let any of this increase in fame go to their heads. When admiring children and adults gathered around and asked to pet the horse, or queried Debra about whether he liked apples or carrots, how fast he liked to go, whether horses slept standing up, or any number of other matters, both Major and his cheerful owner carried on with the same humility and kindness they had shown from the beginning.

River quickly made her planned rounds. At the gallery, Sara was busy with a customer, so River gave Sara a wave and let herself into the workroom to pick up the big box of new signs. She was sorry to not get to chat with Sara; they hadn't really had an opportunity to talk much lately. It would be nice having her in the family soon.

At the café, River had to park some distance away and carry the awkward box of signs, because all the parking nearby was full. A group of people were getting out of the carriage, and another group waited to get into it.

She put the box of signs behind the downstairs counter for Nick to deal with, paid Della for the lunches, and left with three small pie boxes. On her return, River stopped her car in front of the woodworking shop, leaving it just long enough to run the food inside. Both Danny and Kate were busy with customers, so River waved and set their two lunch boxes on the counter.

Back at River Carter's Pottery Works, River unlocked the door with one hand and turned the sign back to "open," clutching the lunch box to her ribs with her other hand. She wondered how many customers *she* had missed while she'd been out. Everyone else's shop certainly had been busy over the noon hour today.

She sat down behind the counter and opened her box of pot pie.

## *Chapter* Fifteen

IN THE TIME since Major the horse had begun making his daily passenger route between the Bowers' bed and breakfast and the café each morning, the B&B had undergone quite a transformation.

No-VOC paint in an elegant, subtle yellow, chosen to be welcoming and mood-lifting for their guests, had been applied to the walls of the new breakfast area, set off by a dove-white color on the trim. Fresh toile curtains in muted colors now graced all of the windows. And in the new gathering room, neutral-colored jute rugs had been placed on the hardwood floors. Several sturdy wooden rocking chairs, handmade by Danny, took their places in groupings with overstuffed furniture, next to conversation tables and baskets filled with books and word games. Tasteful wall décor and other accents gave the room a charming feel that Mrs. Bowers was fairly certain would translate into repeat business.

The Bowers' debate over what to rename the B&B had ended quite abruptly, when they had suddenly and unexpectedly come upon a name they both thought was ideal.

As it happened, while shopping for new décor pieces for the B&B, Mrs. Bowers found herself drawn to a display of various vintage-looking lanterns. And Mr. Bowers, still drawn to Mrs. Bowers after a number of years of marriage, had followed.

Mrs. Bowers had always loved lanterns. She had never thought of herself as a collector, but had perhaps become an accidental collector, just because she liked them.

As the couple took in the display, Mr. Bowers suggested that, since she enjoyed them so much, perhaps they might use lanterns as a signature item in the décor of the reinvented B&B, and even have a lantern in its new logo.

It was moments like this in life, thought Mrs. Bowers, that were not celebrated enough. Those moments when one person honors some spark of light in another that perhaps neither of them understands or names, and just the recognition of it translates into an expression of being known and loved.

Animated by the idea, the pair spontaneously began tossing around some lantern-inspired monikers for their business, and by the time they had arrived home with decorative lanterns of all sizes and descriptions, had decided they both liked *The Old Lantern Inn.*

They'd seen River's new sign at the pottery shop, liked the idea of a metal cutout sign as she'd done, and decided to get the same kind—except with theirs featuring a lantern, of course, and a different typestyle for the lettering.

"When you two get an idea, you don't let any grass grow under your feet, do you?" laughed Natalie a few days later when she stopped by to see her parents' progress at the B&B. "So, I guess this means I can stop thinking about names, naming contests, and all of that?"

"You might as well," said her father. "We've already ordered the sign. It will be installed on Tuesday."

## *Chapter* Sixteen

SNUG IN LAYERED sweaters, warm pants, thick socks, and house shoes, Vera Stanford was taking a break from her writing work to do nothing. She had been creating long enough to know that minds, like fields, sometimes needed to lie fallow in order to regenerate their productivity. And she needed rest.

And so, without any more guilt than one would have over taking the time to brush one's teeth, Vera made a hot drink, took herself to the warmest room of her old house, nestled into a comfortable chair, tucked a blanket around her legs, and *was.*

And then, as often happens when the mind is allowed to rest in such a way, Vera spontaneously received a lovely gift: the idea for her next book.

She had thought she might write a children's book next, but that is not what came. Book ideas, like best friends, Vera had found, often suggested their own arrivals, and were always equally welcome.

Her recent discussion with River about C.S. Lewis's body of work had probably been a seed lying on the ground of her mind, germinating, and then, given the right conditions—a state of rest and quiet—had finally emerged where she could see it.

The contour of that one life, thought Vera, had undoubtedly been instrumental in shaping a generation—at times invisibly, and at other times, quite openly, as Lewis pushed against the work of the spirits of the age. It intrigued her. And what shaping effect had his one life and his work had on subsequent generations, faced with different issues, different spiritual battles?

Ideas sparked in her, and their fibers connected with each other, beginning to form a small tapestry. She would write about the literary legacy of C.S. Lewis from a perspective that—she thought—hadn't been fully written about yet. Some research was definitely in order to make sure, but Vera was enlivened at the possibilities.

This was one of Vera's very favorite parts of the creative process. She loved the genesis of an idea. Of course, she also loved every other part of the process, as well.

Vera resisted the urge to put down her mug and go directly to her study and begin working on the new project.

As exciting as it was, and as eager as she was to jump into it, she wasn't done with her day of rest.

∂∘∂

In another old house in the Valley of Artisans, on the evening of that same day, River Carter was also trying to do nothing.

Her day had been packed nonstop from before sunrise until the Pottery Works closed with all of the tasks of running her two businesses. Now, it was her time to relax.

She had changed into comfortable sweats, heated herself some of the beef stew that Aunt Della had sent home last night with Nick, and turned on soft music.

To an outside observer, it would have appeared that River was relaxing. Except she wasn't at all.

Her mind kept offering up a cornucopia of matters clamoring for her attention. She needed to do laundry. The clean dishes in the kitchen weren't putting themselves away. The floors at her house hadn't been vacuumed since... when? She hadn't gotten the mail today. The utility bills needed to be paid. She needed to get Christmas gifts for nearly everyone on her list. She still needed to figure out *what* to get for nearly everyone on her list.

Before she had even finished eating her soup, River began walking around the house, working through the to-dos on her chaotic mental checklist: she put away dishes, started laundry, paid bills.

*Looks like I'm low on laundry soap. I need to start a shopping list.*

*Is that my last stamp? When am I going to start paying all my bills online? Oh, logins and passwords—that's why I'm not. Wouldn't I have written those down somewhere when I set them up? Oh, well, I'll just go by the post office tomorrow and get more stamps.*

*The mail!*

She pulled on her coat, jammed her shoes into her unlaced winter boots, leaving them untied, and clomped out to the mailbox. Here were two more envelopes with contents demanding her attention, and a Christmas card from a relative on her mom's side of the family in Tennessee.

*Oh, no! I need to send some Christmas cards! And I don't even have any yet.*

She took the mail inside and gave it the consideration it required, and then wrote out a list of who she wanted to send cards to, so she'd know how many she needed to buy.

*Well, this night is shot. Might as well vacuum now, too.*

Her soup had gotten cold. She continued to eat it in snatches while she whirred around the house, vacuuming at top speed.

She put the vacuum cleaner away, turned on the outside light for Nick, brushed her teeth, and went to bed. It was an hour past her usual bedtime. Her body felt like she'd been in high gear all day and all evening, and was still going 25 over the speed limit.

She would do this better tomorrow night. She would come home, she would really relax, and anything she thought of that needed doing would just have to wait. Except that she did need to buy those Christmas cards and get them ready.

Just then River remembered she'd left her empty soup bowl on the counter. She got up and rinsed it and set it in the sink.

Sometime after midnight, River finally got to sleep.

# *Chapter* Seventeen

NATALIE BOWERS KNEW this wasn't a good time of year to call a special meeting of the Guild, but it couldn't be helped. And so, in the email she sent out the following morning, she apologized to the Guild members for the inconvenience, but stressed the necessity of their gathering that same evening to vote on a matter of great importance.

Since Natalie wasn't in the habit of crying wolf, River knew that something big really must be going on. Maybe she would still have time to get her Christmas cards and write them tonight, if the Guild meeting didn't take too long, River thought, as she brushed her hair and chose a turtleneck sweater for the day.

*Maybe I could run out at lunch and get some cards from that shop down the street that sells the handmade ones. But do I really want to miss out on potential lunchtime business?*

As it turned out, River didn't have to make the choice. Danny called. He had a new batch of blank signs ready, which Sara needed at her shop today to fill internet orders already in hand. Kate had driven to the city to pick up some supplies Danny needed for the woodworking shop and wouldn't be back until time for the Guild meeting, and Danny couldn't leave the shop because he had a tour group arriving. Could River take the blanks over to Sara? Sara's shop was too busy for her to leave it, she had told Danny.

River looked around her own shop. There were groups of customers browsing in every aisle. Well, she would just have to turn her sign around to *Closed*, wait until all of these customers left, and then make the run herself. It couldn't be helped. She'd come straight back, and reopen as soon as humanly possible.

On her way to Sara's gallery, River drove past the shop that sold the handmade Christmas cards. She peered at the sign to see how late it was open. Same closing time as hers. So much for the handmade Christmas cards. And she'd have to go straight to the Guild meeting when she closed the

Pottery Works, or else she'd be late for that. She'd just have to go somewhere else to get cards after the Guild meeting was over.

❧❦

That evening, Guild members from all over town converged at the duly appointed meeting place, eager to hear what was so urgent, and also eager to get home to a warm dinner after a long day—and not necessarily in that order, in every case.

Natalie Bowers began the meeting right on time. She said the matter at hand was an opportunity for the Valley of Artisans to gain increased visibility during WinterFest, but also came with a deadline and a cost. That, she said, was why they needed to hear and decide on the matter so quickly.

The magazine of a *high-profile lifestyle personality*, Natalie said, had contacted the Guild. River wondered if it might one day be back in fashion to just say *person*, instead of *personality*.

The magazine was inviting the Valley of Artisans to be part of its January/February feature,

*100 Cool Places to Go When It's Cold.* The list would showcase lesser-known tourist areas from each state that fit the type of creative, down-to-earth life this brand was promoting—and that had not already been featured in the magazine's November/December issue list of *Close-to-Home Holiday Destinations.*

The magazine apologized for the short notice, Natalie read, but had decided to expand its list to include more attractions than originally planned. The deadline hadn't changed, however, so if the Valley of Artisans wished to be included, it would need to return the required application, and a not-insignificant sum of money, by yesterday, if possible. Slots were filling up fast, and so on.

The air was charged with excitement. Wasn't this exactly the kind of thing that could turn a little place few people had ever heard of, into a destination? And wasn't the readership of this *high-profile lifestyle personality* a match with the type of people who usually enjoyed the Valley of Artisans and became repeat visitors? It was serendipitous. Not cheap, but certainly it would be worth the investment, wouldn't it? Wouldn't the expenditure bring returns many times over?

River leaned over and whispered to Kate.

"What do you think?"

"I'm really leaning towards yes," said Kate. "How about you?"

River couldn't see a downside, and wondered if—other than the cost—there was one.

"Me, too," said River.

River looked around the room at those assembled, scanning the room for anyone who appeared to be less excited than the rest. It was then she realized that Mr. Lyle wasn't at the meeting.

When the Guild had concluded its business by all in favor indicating so by saying "aye," and the ayes having it, River and Kate gathered their things and walked out together.

"Danny still working?" River asked.

"Yes, that tour group today put him behind a couple of hours in the shop. But he had such a good time showing them how things are made, that he didn't even mind," she laughed.

"Well, that's good, at least," said River.

"He said when he saw you today, it seemed like you were meeting yourself coming and going," said Kate with an inquiring look at her friend's face.

"It's kind of been like that lately, now that you mention it," said River. "Which reminds me, I still have to get Christmas cards tonight. I'd better get going."

"Alright, well, enjoy this last little bit of anonymity while you can," called Kate playfully, as the two diverged to go to their separate cars, "because once that magazine article comes out, we'll both be so famous we probably won't even be able to go to a store, or even get our mail, without the paparazzi snapping photos."

"Ha, ha," replied River, as her friend closed her car door.

River got into her own cold car, started it, and closed all the vents to keep the not-yet-warm air from blowing on her. She hoped the coming publicity would continue to build tourism and sales in the Valley, but she seriously doubted it would impede her from getting her own mail.

She tried to think of someplace within close driving distance that would still be open that would have the kind of cards she wanted to send. Or any cards at all.

◈

River's quest for Christmas cards had been successful. Once her dinner was eaten, she had sat at the kitchen table, listening to her favorite Christmas harp music playing, writing and addressing cards. She wanted to have them all ready to take to the post office tomorrow at lunch time.

And so, while River would typically have been asleep long before her brother got home from the café, on that night, he found her awake and still writing cards when he came in.

"River, you amaze me," said her brother, pulling out a kitchen chair to sit down.

River laughed. "What's amazing about writing Christmas cards after midnight?"

"No, not that. It's just—your whole life here. You've taken on so much and run with it well."

"You really think so?" asked River, surprised at Nick's observation.

"Yeah. I do."

*Hm. Well, if Nick, who knows me as well as anyone, thinks I am handling things well, then maybe I am.*

River took her brother's comment to heart, and found it useful for buoying her up. She didn't *quite* feel like a drowning woman, but lately it had seemed as if the water was consistently just below her nostrils.

## *Chapter* Eighteen

JIM HADN'T BEEN trying to be antisocial, but his sister Della had noticed that he had been quieter than usual.

Oh, well, she thought, he had a lot to do and a lot to think about, with preparing to get married and move—not to mention the task of combining two complete households.

While all of that was true, it was also true that Jim *had* been quieter than he would have been if he hadn't also been trying to wrestle with the great divide that had come between Sara and him.

Jim had decided that probably nothing could *close* the gap, but he'd been wondering if there were a way to *bridge* it. He hoped so. He didn't agree with Sara that anything was still open for miracles. But at the same time, he loved her too much to let this difference come between them.

After all, he thought, this disagreement was like two people who have never seen the dark side of the moon being at complete odds over what was there. What was the difference? What did it matter, really, to their lives?

And so, as Jim pulled some summer clothes out of his bedroom closet that night and folded them into a moving box, he arrived at a decision: He *could* believe differently than Sara on this point, and still be married to her.

೧∾ಌ

While Jim was busy packing, Sara was busy painting.

The workroom at the back of her gallery had been a very busy place for days on end now, but Sara didn't mind that. Working late had given her the time she needed to think.

And what she thought was that maybe she had been too judgmental of Jim's position. After all, didn't they say marriage is about compromise? And wasn't this probably exactly the kind of thing about which compromise might be required?

She knew she truly loved Jim, and she believed he really loved her. *Surely*, she thought, as she washed out some brushes at the work sink, watching the distinct, bright colors mingle into a muddy swirl at the bottom, *we can sort out how our different approaches to faith can work together.*

# *Chapter* Nineteen

IT WAS THAT point during the busy shopping season when all Valley of Artisans shopkeepers were working at maximum capacity.

Privately, they were each encouraged by the increase in sales they were seeing over the previous year—their efforts were paying off. However, the initial burst of adrenaline of the start of WinterFest had worn off, and the business owners were now grinding their metaphorical engines into second gear to make it the rest of the way up the hill.

And so, it was a welcome boost to the entire membership of the Guild to receive some unexpected good news in an email from their leader, Natalie Bowers. Natalie had first, however, phoned her parents, since the news concerned the B&B in a primary way.

The same magazine that had invited the Valley of Artisans to be part of its January/February *100*

*Cool Places to Go When It's Cold* article had just emailed her. The magazine had decided to feature a photo of the Valley of Artisans' B&B on the front cover of its January/February issue, *Warm Welcomes in Winter*. The cover would show The Old Lantern Inn, with the horse and carriage sitting out front.

"Well, but how much is *this* going to cost?" Mrs. Bowers had asked.

Natalie scanned the email again, mumbling half-words as she did.

"Here it is," she said. "'There is no fee for this additional exposure.'"

"Just think!" Natalie continued, "Your B&B is going to be seen nationally."

"Sounds like we got that new sign just in time," said Mr. Bowers.

## *Chapter* Twenty

VERA HAD BROUGHT home a stack of research material from the library—two or three stacks, in fact—and was presently absorbed in a refresher study. She had scheduled no outside engagements for this week, because there were times, she had learned, when her thoughts needed their own quiet space.

So many different kinds of writing had characterized the career of C.S. Lewis—it was a varied tapestry, to be sure. But Vera was following a certain strand among those threads: the way in which, through much of his work, Lewis's words acted like hands shaping the thinking of a generation.

Lewis's own *life*, Vera had long observed, had been a study in that same type of formation.

In his private writing as a young adult, Lewis had once made critical remarks about one of his aunts, regarding her perception of the closeness of her relationship with God, and her dogmatic stance on a popular ethical issue of the day. Not knowing that lady personally, Vera wondered if Lewis's impressions had been accurate—and the woman truly *had* been an exhausting clanging cymbal—or whether she had actually been one of the lifelines God brings into the life of an unbeliever.

Even though that aunt hadn't been the believer through whom Lewis's conversion to Christ had come, Vera thought it might have been possible that the woman's words had perhaps planted a seed, or watered it. Or maybe, Vera thought, it had been entirely the opposite. That woman's manner of speaking about God and the things she considered important to God might have been so off-putting to Lewis so as to be an obstacle.

It was either an encouragement or a cautionary tale, thought Vera, and she did not have enough objective information to know which. Either way, she couldn't help noticing that Lewis's own writing later addressed the very same popular ethical issue of the day that his aunt had cared so much about, and he repeatedly explored the outer reaches of his own relationship with the very same God.

Where Vera wanted to shine light now was on how creative work and spirits of the age pushed against each other, in the conflict between two spiritual kingdoms.

Vera had long been a reader of literature written in previous centuries. She had repeatedly taken special notice of the way spirits were influential in shaping people's thoughts and lives, and the structures of society. These issues—different from one century to the next, and even from one generation to the next—seemed to form a kind of container, she perceived, in which writers lived and wrote—whether or not they acknowledged that reality in their writing, and whether or not they were even aware of it themselves.

Her task now was to illuminate how Lewis's work—so beloved—was itself affected by such influences—and pushed back against them.

*A new generation of writers is always coming up,* thought Vera, *and their words are not just toy swords being waved in the air for fun. The sooner their eyes are opened to the spiritual reality surrounding them, the better prepared they will be to bring God's kingdom near.*

Vera Stanford thought no more highly—or less—of herself than she should. But she hoped—and expected—that her work would be part of that. She was part of a family, and of a body. Every part was different, every part was needed. And she knew that she was doing what she had been created to do.

Vera leaned forward in her chair and wrote.

## *Chapter* Twenty-One

EARLIER IN THE month, River had envisioned
going on a fun Christmas gift shopping excursion
with Kate, but it didn't look like there would be
time for that.

In fact, River realized she didn't even really
have time for *any* type of shopping excursion—
fun or not.

She liked to shop local and she wanted to
support creative work, so she did her best at both
by visiting the websites of the other Guild
members in the Valley of Artisans and ordering
items online. Many offered the option of local
pickup, which she also liked. By the time she had
completed her Christmas shopping late one night
at the kitchen table, she felt she had done the best
she could. She hoped she could make her rounds
of all the pickups in a single lunch hour, in order
to avoid having to close her pottery shop over the
noontime any more than necessary and miss out

on making sales of her own during the busy shopping season.

*Next year*, she thought, *I need to do more holiday preparation earlier—like in the summer.*

It sounded good, but she wondered if she would follow through with this intention. There were benefits to planning ahead, of course, but wasn't there also something to be said for living in the flow of the seasons as they actually happened?

Was the only way to make December livable to live part of that winter month in July? Then what summer things would she miss out on?

She wondered how other shop owners were making their lives work during WinterFest. She made a mental note to ask Aunt Della how *she* did everything.

River would have a minor shock waiting for her when she did. Aunt Della had, over the years, found that the secret to getting everything done was to *not do everything*. One needed to pick and choose in life, she would tell her great-niece, when and if she ever asked.

## *Chapter* Twenty-Two

ONE THING RIVER'S great-aunt Della *hadn't* done was develop a gluten-free menu at the café, even when she knew the day was coming that a customer would ask for one.

As it turned out, that day was at hand.

The town's oldest physician, Doc Gregory, had gotten wind of the fuss that Mr. Lyle had caused at the recent Guild meetings. Words spoken anywhere within the Valley of Artisans tended to get carried in all directions, as a predictable breeze distributed them.

And so, when Jake Lyle, who was just a few years younger than Doc Gregory—which they both well knew, because Jake Lyle's older sister had been in Doc's class at high school—came in for his yearly checkup, Doc asked his patient if he was feeling grumpier than was usual for him.

Mr. Lyle thought about the question. It was hard to say. That was a difficult thing to measure from the inside, but the more he considered it, he realized he *had* been rather more sick and tired of himself lately. He answered accordingly.

The nurse practitioner, who had grown up in the town and was familiar with the patient, silently entered a note into the computer at which he sat in the corner of the room.

Doc Gregory, who was a seasoned outdoorsman in addition to being a medical professional, knew a thing or two about not scaring off his quarry.

He nonchalantly addressed Mr. Lyle.

"Well, *I* think you should just count your blessings that you have blessings to count. There *are* some lifestyle changes you could try if you wanted to," said Doc. "Mind you, probably none of them will work, but it won't be my time you're wasting. Just suit yourself; you will anyway."

The young nurse practitioner swallowed a snort and hid a laugh inside a sudden loud cough, as the wily old doctor continued.

"I'll have Ben here print you the list," said the doctor, writing a note for the nurse. "But don't count on any of it making a hill of beans of difference, and don't come complaining to me when it doesn't. I don't get paid enough for that."

The old doctor's tactics had hit their mark. Mr. Lyle set his jaw right then to do these so-called *lifestyle changes*, whatever they were. He had never been one to do much of anything beyond what the law and his business required of a person. He wasn't sure he even *had* a *lifestyle*—or knew what that might include, for that matter.

"You come back in six months," said the old doctor, standing up from his rolling stool and handing his notes to the nurse. "I don't want to see you before then."

Without waiting for a reply, Doc Gregory strode out of the room.

He had played his role to a T.

Mr. Lyle waited impatiently as Ben printed out the information the doctor had indicated. He snatched the papers out of the young nurse's hands as soon as they had been lifted from the printer.

He'd just see about this.

Mr. Lyle was still reading over the printouts from the doctor as he waited in line at the busy café. He didn't remember ever having to wait for a table here before. He looked around and saw many unfamiliar faces. Maybe this WinterFest thing was doing something, after all. He certainly hoped so, for all the trouble and expense it had been.

When Della seated him, Mr. Lyle asked for the gluten-free menu.

"Well, now, Mr. Lyle, I don't have one, but I could bring you a hot vegetable plate or a green salad," she said.

"Is there gluten in any of that?" he asked.

"No, no gluten at all," Della replied. She couldn't remember what gluten was, but she knew it was something in grain, and she knew she put no grain in her vegetable dishes.

"I'll take one of each, then. I'll show that old Doc Gregory what's what."

"Coming right up," said Della, turning on one foot and heading straight into the kitchen to give Nick the order.

"Nick," said his aunt, leaning in and speaking in undertones, "I think we may need to develop a gluten-free menu. It sounds like Doc Gregory has begun handing out some dietary changes."

Nick laughed.

"No problem, Aunt Della. We covered all kinds of special diets in school. I can easily get a menu together for that." As he talked, he continued to cook and plate orders.

"Good," said Della. "Because I don't have the first idea how to make anything gluten-free if isn't born that way or grown that way to begin with."

"Don't you worry; consider it covered," said her great-nephew with a reassuring smile.

Not for the first time, Della silently thanked God for sending her Nick. She pushed open the kitchen door and went back to the dining room to check on her customers.

## *Chapter* Twenty-Three

AS THE DECEMBER days continued to fly by, Sara and Jim tried to carry on with the joy a couple might rightly expect to feel during a happy engagement. But instead of buoyancy, both of them felt pulled down by a heavy weight.

Neither could deny the strain of the uneasy truces they had each made with themselves. It just wasn't working. There was no contention between them, just bare desperation to find a way for them to go forward *together*.

Knowing they had to do something, they agreed to try discussing the issue again.

"Jim, I need you to help me understand," Sara began softly, "how it is possible for a follower of Christ to arrive at the conclusion you hold.

"I am not accusing you, and I am not berating you," she continued earnestly. "I'm really *asking*. Jesus performed all kinds of signs and miracles, and a book about the things he did was *written* so *we would* believe. Can you help me understand how it is that you don't?"

"Have you ever seen one?" Jim asked her quietly. "An actual miracle, I mean."

"No, I haven't," said Sara. And then, in the same gentle tone, "But is that conclusive proof that there can't be any? Don't we both believe things we haven't seen?"

Jim was silent.

Again, they had reached that same invisible wall between them, and neither knew how to get over it, around it, or through it.

They sat in Sara's living room without speaking.

After some time, a new thought occurred to Sara, and she quietly spoke it aloud.

"Jim, what if something happens in our lives and *we* need a miracle—you, or me, or both of us? You won't even *ask* for one."

"That's true," said Jim.

"And," Sara continued slowly, "maybe worse—but I'm not sure—you'll think it's pointless—or maybe even *wrong*—for *me or anyone else* to pursue one."

It seemed that, even after talking repeatedly, openly, with love and respect, about this issue, the couple still found themselves at an impasse.

"So, what do we do?" Sara asked Jim, her sad eyes brimming with tears.

"I don't know, Sara," said Jim. "I know we love each other, and I want us to find a way to make this work."

"I do, too, Jim," Sara said. "I just don't know how to do that."

❧

Late that evening, after Nick had left the café for the day, a weary Jim sat at his sister Della's kitchen table. The two shared the remains of a pot of coffee that had no doubt tasted good sometime much earlier that day, as Jim told his lifelong confidante about his problem.

"You were married," he said, after explaining the matter. "What do you think about this? I could use some advice."

"Well," said his sister, "if this is an issue for you and Sara now, it won't be automatically resolved by a signed marriage certificate. It's something both of you are going to have to come to terms with in *some* way."

Jim thought for a few silent minutes, as Della patiently sat across from him.

"I've been trying to accept that it would be okay for us to believe differently about this," Jim said, "but I'm just not feeling right about going ahead with the marriage while things are this way. I want her to able to walk down the aisle with *joy*—not the burden of questions and feelings she's carrying right now. I think I need to suggest to Sara that we postpone the wedding while we sort this out."

☙❧

A short distance away in the Valley, Sara was sitting up in the dark of her own living room, thinking, while the antique mantel clock chimed every quarter hour.

*My love for Jim is not in question*, she thought. *But if he really doesn't believe miracles are possible, then has he barricaded off parts of himself to the work of God? How can the life of God be fully at work in him? How* can I enter this marriage—a joining of my life with his—when that's the way I see things?

In the end, even if she couldn't answer her questions about Jim, it was her own obvious lack of peace that led her to the decision she knew she had to make.

I can't go through with this marriage.

Sara was upset with herself for not realizing all of this much earlier. Making the decision now to call off the wedding would cause everyone, including herself, much pain. Pain she was already feeling like a stabbing and crushing of her own heart.

But how could she have known to look out for something she didn't even know existed? She had had no idea that there were believers who even believed that way.

It's as if I am a bird and he is a fish, she thought. We just can't find a place where we can exist together and both breathe.

I can't do anything about that now, Sara told herself. All I can do now is decide how to move forward. And without peace, I can't go ahead with the marriage.

# *Chapter* Twenty-Four

EARLY THE NEXT morning, Sara's phone rang. It was Jim, asking if he could come by for just a few minutes to talk before she had to leave for the gallery.

Sara's eyes looked puffy and red, Jim noticed, as he sat down at her kitchen table.

"I know we're at an impasse right now about something that isn't working for us," Jim began, "and I wonder if it would take the pressure off of us if we were to postpone the wedding just until we can figure out how to resolve this."

*That was kind*, thought Sara. *Kind, but not a solution.*

"Jim, as much as I wish that could be our answer, I think we would just be postponing the inevitable," Sara gently replied. "I know we love and respect each other and that we want to work this out, but we've already tried. I just don't see a way forward for us to the future we wanted together."

Jim involuntarily took a quick, shallow breath. He couldn't believe it had come to this. But here it was. They were no longer talking about postponing the wedding; they were calling off *everything*. He felt the clock of his life momentarily stop. He tried to swallow, but the muscles of his throat wouldn't move.

Finally, when he could speak again, he told Sara he knew she was right. And that he loved her. And that he was truly sorry for the way things had ended up.

Jim said he couldn't believe they were actually talking about their relationship *ending*, when he had looked forward to spending the rest of his life with her.

Sara just shook her head and hugged Jim. She was crying too hard to talk, but there was nothing else to say, anyway. It had taken them more than half a lifetime to find each other. And now, in the space of about 10 minutes, they had gone from an engaged couple planning to wed in less than a month, to two people who would just happen to live in the same town. Both of their lives had been stretched larger—in the best way—to make room for each other. But now they were snapping back to their original size—unexpectedly, painfully.

Neither felt in any condition to go to work, but both knew they had to. And so, they said goodbye and drove away from Sara's house, he, toward the café, and she, toward her gallery.

When Sara arrived, she opened her business as usual and then went into the work room at the back to make a phone call—one of the first of many that she and Jim would have to place to their families and friends.

Her call was to Marian at the wedding chapel, to let her know that her business's first couple wouldn't be coming down the aisle after all.

"Oh, Sara, I'm really sad for both of you. Truly."

Then, after a pause, Marian continued, in a tone that Sara was sure was meant to be encouraging.

"Okay, Sara, I want you to know that I am hearing you, but I'm also leaving your wedding on the books. These things often have a way of turning around."

"Thank you, Marian," Sara sighed, "but I think it would take a miracle at this point."

## *Chapter* Twenty-Five

IT WAS LATE morning, and River had left the wheel at her shop to attend to several customers. She had just finished helping the last one, when more came in. She loved selling pottery, but at this rate, she wasn't going to have time to throw enough new pottery to keep up. She had counted on being able to make a certain number of pieces each day during business hours.

*Smile and sell,* she told herself. *You won't fix anything by worrying about it.*

Just then, her phone vibrated on the counter. It was a text from Nick: *We need to talk ASAP. I'm coming over.*

*What?,* thought River. *It's the start of lunch on a weekday over there. Shouldn't Nick be busy helping Della with the cooking and serving right now?*

River hoped everything was alright.

She didn't have long to wait before finding out that it wasn't.

When Nick came in, seeing the Pottery Works full of customers, he walked toward the open doorway of her workroom. She followed. He began speaking in a hushed voice.

"Uncle Jim came into the café today and told Aunt Della and me that he and Sara have called off the wedding."

"They've *what?!*"

Two customers looked up from their shopping. River smiled and nodded at them. "Just let me know if I can help you with anything," she said in a friendly tone to the prospective buyers.

Nick continued quietly.

"I don't know the details, but they've definitely broken up. Which also means Uncle Jim's not going anywhere."

"But, what about you?"

"Well, I really don't think that business can support a third person, so it doesn't look like I'll be moving here to work at the café, after all. I'll just have to get another job somewhere else."

"Oh, Nick," his sister groaned. "This was all so perfect for you. It was what you wanted, and it was working out so well."

"I know, Riv. I don't know what happened, but it sounds like all of Humpty Dumpty's men aren't going to get this thing back together again."

"I am so sorry, Nick," said River. "I don't know which I hate more—their relationship being broken up, or your life being upended like this. I guess I don't have to pick—I can hate both, right?"

"Well, there's more," said Nick.

Just then, a customer approached the counter tentatively with one of the winter mugs in her hand.

"Yes," said River brightly to the woman.

"I was wondering if you would have twelve of these. I'd like to have a dozen matching ones, but I only saw seven on the shelf."

"Let me go check in the back," said River.

She stepped past her brother, who was patiently leaning against the doorway to the workroom. He gave her customer a friendly smile.

*His life is imploding, and here he is, thinking about being gracious to my customers*, thought River.

She was glad to see that she did have just enough of the mug design in question on the rack of finished pottery in the back to fill the woman's request. However, selling all of this design also meant she urgently needed to make more of them.

After helping that customer and then another behind her who was ready to check out, River returned to Nick.

"Sorry. You said there was more. What else?" she said.

"Well, River, I'm sorry, but all this means that I won't be around to take care of the Signs and Wonders store at the café."

River nodded slowly, understanding sinking in. It looked as if the new retail brick-and-mortar location of Signs and Wonders would be a short-lived venture.

At the moment, however, any feelings River had about that were overshadowed by her concern for her brother, for her great-uncle, and for Sara.

This was a sad day for the dreams of the people she loved.

"I need to get back to the café," said Nick, "but I just wanted to tell you in person."

"Nick, what will you do?"

"I'll stay here through the holidays, or until I find another job. Jim may be at the café, but he's also a million miles away, if you know what I mean. I think he's going to need a little time to get back to himself. But I'll start applying right away for other jobs."

River sighed heavily.

"Hey, at least I haven't already unpacked—with nearly all my stuff in boxes in your garage, I'm ready to move anywhere," said Nick.

River hated to think about her brother leaving. It had been so great to have him here in the Valley, even though they hadn't been able to spend much time together.

"Okay, we'll talk more later," she said. "I know you have to get back."

Nick jogged out to his car and headed back to the café and a line of hungry customers.

River sat down at the counter, where she'd be ready to help her shoppers check out.

She knew there wasn't enough profit margin in the sign business to *hire* someone to take Nick's place at Signs and Wonders. And she wouldn't dream of asking Aunt Della and Uncle Jim to take on anything extra. They would probably say yes at this point, but she would never feel right about it.

Their hands were full running the café and keeping up two households. And if they had felt like climbing those stairs, they'd probably be using the upstairs space for the café.

Not to mention, River thought sadly, Uncle Jim's heart would probably be broken for a good while to come.

But what *were* they going to do about the sign shop? There hadn't been space at the woodworking shop, Sara's gallery, or the Pottery Works to display the Signs and Wonders inventory even back when it was only online. There *really* wasn't now, since they had increased production to make more inventory for the brick-and-mortar store. They needed an additional space for the sign shop to call its own.

As soon as there was a lull, River called Kate to let her and Danny know the news about the sign business—and the reason for it.

"We don't have to make a decision right away. Nick is going to stay until he finds another job. So, he can keep running Signs and Wonders for now. But we will have to make some decisions pretty soon."

"Okay, River, we understand," said Kate. "And we're sure sorry for Jim and Sara. I wonder if Jim will even want to still do the accounting for Signs and Wonders if he's going back to working at the café, you know? It might be too much, with only so many hours in the day."

"Yeah, good question," said River.

The bell over the door jangled as a customer walked in.

"Gotta go," said River. "Talk later."

"Yep, bye," said Kate.

River greeted her customer and kindly guided her to the items she'd asked about. As River returned to the counter, she stopped and stared out the front window, looking at nothing.

Although she hadn't let herself see it before, she now realized that the demands of the sign business *had* been a drain on her lately. And, judging from the state of the inventory shelf in her pottery shop, it had been a drag on her core business, too. She wasn't keeping up with the work she so loved. More than just not keeping up, though, she felt she was being stretched, to a thinness that didn't leave enough room for life to flow in her the way she wanted.

Yet, instead of experiencing *relief* at the idea of having to close the brick-and-mortar location of Signs and Wonders—as she might have expected, given the resistance she had been feeling about it—the idea of saying goodbye to the physical store, now that it had actually sprung to life, created a sense of real loss.

River didn't even understand her own mixed feelings. How could she figure out the right way to move forward making decisions about the sign business, if she was already this confused? She couldn't very well drag Danny, Kate, and Sara along on a ride she didn't even want to be on. But what if she *did* want to be on it? The only way she *could* do it was *with them*.

She needed to figure this out, and soon.

# *Chapter* Twenty-Six

CLOUDS COVERED THE sun all day.

Jim sat on the couch in his house and stared at his phone.

Della had suggested that Jim take some time to make his calls, and then maybe get some rest and come eat dinner with them in the kitchen later before the evening rush. She assured her brother that she and Nick had lunch service covered.

Deciding the matter between Sara and himself was one thing, but once they started telling wedding guests not to come because there was no wedding, it would be as over-and-done as a thing could be. And if he had ever wanted to *not* do a thing, ending this relationship was it.

*If only I could see things the way Sara does*, Jim thought, *we wouldn't be going through this heartache. But how can I believe what I've never seen?*

Sara usually took lunch with her to the gallery, but that morning, of course, hadn't been usual. And so, she closed her gallery just long enough to make the quick trip home to pick up the soup and fruit she'd packed but forgotten in the refrigerator.

As she hurried back out of the house to her idling car, lunch tote cradled in one arm, she looked at the furniture and stacks of boxes filling her garage—the material evidence of two lives that had tried to mesh into one.

Just a few days ago, this had all still been part of an exciting transition. Now it was just a big mess to be cleaned up.

She felt so much loss that her heart physically hurt.

*But what can I do?* Sara thought, as she pulled away.

෯෯

At the café, Della went about her work, feeling that her world was shifting yet again. She chatted in a friendly way with her customers, as always, but felt a constant ache for her heartbroken brother. Jim and Sara had seemed like such a happy match, and had been so elated. And now it was all over.

Della was caught up in her thoughts when Mr. Lyle came in for dinner. Without being asked, she brought him one of the new gluten-free menus Nick had created—significantly expanded from the options Della had originally offered Mr. Lyle— and a regular menu. *She* wasn't his doctor—he could order what he wanted. Della asked the town's typically surly broomsquire how he was doing.

"Oh, can't complain, can't complain," Mr. Lyle responded, almost cheerily.

Sometimes the world was just upside down and backwards, thought Della.

## *Chapter* Twenty-Seven

"IT'S SO HARD to sort out, it feels like someone has dumped out the pieces of two different puzzles into the same pile," said River to her friend Vera, when they had both sat down in the study at Vera's house. They normally visited at the kitchen table, but it was a cold day today, and Vera said this was the warmest place in the house right now.

Vera had started some water heating for tea, and had barely gotten back to the room before River jumped into the deep end of the conversational pool, telling her friend about how Jim and Sara's wedding being called off had led to Nick's plans to depart the café—and the sign shop, and to River's deepening dilemma over her involvement in the Signs and Wonders business.

Vera remained silent as she listened to her friend.

"I'm so confused," said River. "Why didn't I feel happier about that new sign store that everyone else was so excited about—and that I should be excited about, too?" She seemed to not even take a breath as she continued. "And now that it looks like the sign store is going to have to close, why do I feel sad instead of relieved? My feelings don't even make sense."

In the sacred space that somehow always existed around Vera, the stream of River's thoughts suddenly took a different, deeper path than the one she had been aware of for the past several weeks. She paused, with a deep breath.

"You know," River said, more slowly, "I originally thought my resistance to opening the physical location of Signs and Wonders was just that my life would be too busy. But I just realized— that wasn't it."

River looked around the quiet room, as if to make sure she and Vera were the only two there before she continued speaking. She realized she was about to trust her friend with some details she hadn't shared before.

"I think I was concerned that adding one more venture would take away from the focus I need to devote to the pottery business to run it well."

Vera remained silent, sensing that her friend was getting close to the root of something, but hadn't quite uncovered it yet.

"Last year," said River, "right after I reopened the pottery shop, I made a pricing error when I set up my online store. It cost me my entire profit margin on a huge chunk of inventory. It was the kind of mistake that could have ended up costing me my fledgling business."

She continued. "But, despite the financial loss from my mistake, the business pulled through, and then grew—thank God."

Vera said nothing.

"The problem is," River went on, "the error wasn't the kind of mistake a person makes from being careless, or in a hurry, or bad at business math. I *wasn't* careless or in a hurry when I worked on those prices—I double-checked them, and I *knew* what I was doing."

"The reason for the mistake was some neurocognitive glitch, leftover from when I had mold illness," she went on. "It made some piece of incorrect logic seem correct in the moment, and my brain did not detect it as an error," River said.

"By the time I moved here last year, I'd recovered to the point that those occurrences were rare for me, but that's what happened."

Vera already knew about the memory problems mold illness had caused River; she had prayed for her friend's complete physical healing last summer when River was sorting through returning memories. But this was the first time River had talked about *this*.

River glanced at Vera's face and was relieved to find acceptance. There were certain things it was just easier to not talk about, and this was one of them. People usually didn't understand unless they had experienced it firsthand.

"The thing is," River continued, "that mistake last year with the pottery business affected only me. But what if I made another one now with the sign business? It wouldn't affect just me, but all of my partners—Danny and Kate, and Sara."

"I guess I just realized that, ever since last summer, I've been waiting for the other shoe to drop. With no warning, I could make another mistake like that that could damage—or end—one of my businesses."

River looked down at her hands. She had done more than expose the truth to Vera. She was facing it herself, as well. Did she have what it would take to succeed in her ventures without failing—and letting others down?

The teakettle whistled. Vera excused herself to make their tea, and said she would be back in a few minutes.

Alone in the study, River sank back into the couch and gazed around her for the first time. Shelves filled with books lined two walls. A writing desk in front of one window was covered with papers, surrounding a computer keyboard and monitor. A work table in front of the other window bore stacks of books, about half of which were opened and nested atop each other.

She recognized that this room where Vera wrote was a sort of sanctum. It reminded her of her workroom in the pottery shop, in a way: quiet, peaceful, yet alive with a thread of energy.

River closed her eyes and thought about the night she and her Signs and Wonders partners had looked through the boxes of Grandma Ella's signs at her house. It had been fun. She had enjoyed being with her new friends in the venture. But how had it compared to the feeling she had when she was creating new pottery designs at her wheel? *It hadn't.*

Was it even fair to ask herself such a question? Why did she have to analyze everything until it sizzled away to ash under the bright light of inquiry?

But River couldn't leave the question alone: *Even if she could make the additional business work— should she?*

She was a little shocked at having had the thought, but wasn't it a fair question?

After all, *pottery* was the business she loved and wanted to be her life's work. Was the new sign store even the *right kind* of pursuit for her? Or was she following too closely in the footsteps of Grandma Ella—who had always loved signs and sayings—by making a business out of what *Ella* loved, rather than forging her own creative path in life—the trail that she, River Carter, had been designed to blaze?

When Vera returned to the room with hot tea for them both, she listened as River poured out her newfound questions about whether the sign business might just be a nostalgic reach into Grandma Ella's past, rather than a pursuit that really belonged in River's future.

Vera and Grandma Ella had been best friends. If anyone could understand missing Ella and wanting part of her to live on, it would be Vera.

"When it comes to finding the right path for one's life," said Vera, "I try to keep in mind that not everything we *can* do, is actually beneficial *to* do."

"That's a good point," said River thoughtfully. "I guess I've been really focused on what I *can* do. But maybe it's not the only criteria for living."

"*Can* and *should* are sometimes light years apart," the older woman said, taking a drink from her steaming mug. "It's really wisdom that is needed where those two are concerned."

"Mm," River replied, swallowing tea. "Okay."

"I have long relied on Proverbs 3:6," said her friend. "In all your ways acknowledge him, and he shall direct your paths."

"I don't think I've been doing that," said River. "I'm not sure what I've been doing, exactly, but it doesn't seem like it's been that."

Vera laughed a friendly laugh.

"And you know," said Vera, "about the other matter—of waiting for a second shoe to drop—instead of expecting and watching for the negative to happen, there is another approach you could take."

"Please," said River, leaning forward, "tell me."

"It's the regular practice of expressing gratitude to God anytime you realize that you are able to now do something that had been lost in your health, and then just telling him what you still need," said Vera. "God promises that that way leads to peace.

"And just like I did when I prayed for your complete physical healing last year," she continued, "*expect* that God is *for* you."

River was more than willing to accept her friend's counsel. She remembered that powerful prayer; it had changed her, somehow, inside. She believed that Vera knew what she was talking about.

"Thank you," said River. "I am definitely going to do these things."

River took in a slow breath and leaned back in her chair. Even before she had all the answers she needed, she knew she had something now that had been missing before.

She began her gratitude practice at that moment, silently thanking God for being *for* her. For being willing to direct her paths when she submitted her ways to him. And for her friend Vera.

The answers would come, thought River. And when they did, she would give thanks for that, too.

## *Chapter* Twenty-Eight

FOR THE FIRST time in her professional life, River had asked God for guidance for her decisions. Now, she was waiting for his answer, and she was determined not to miss it.

She was also taking seriously the practice of gratitude that Vera had advised. As she considered the events of the past several months, River examined her life in detail for *good* rather than *negative*.

She was thankful that during the weeks when she had been handling *two* businesses—her growing pottery business and the fledgling sign business—she hadn't had any neurocognitive glitches like the one that nearly derailed River Carter's Pottery Works at its startup last year. In fact, as River looked back over her calendar at the events of last year, she was surprised to realize that even before opening the online Signs and Wonders business, there hadn't been *any* more glitches. And it had been *months*. She felt a surge of quiet excitement.

It had also been quite a while, she realized, since she had needed to rely on all the memory crutches her brain had still needed when she first moved here. She knew when she'd last picked up her mail. She remembered to put out the trash on the correct day without using the reminder on her phone. She had even been recalling the names of local customers in her shop who'd only been in a time or two—something she never could have done before. She was remembering things normally.

*How had she not realized this sooner?* River wondered. Had her latent fear that another shoe would drop caused her to miss noticing all of these improvements? But there they were. And she knew they were real. Not only had no other *oversized* shoe fallen, but the smaller cognitive tasks of daily living for which she had become so used to needing helps and workarounds also seemed to be normal now, too.

River wasn't sure whether this was how a gratitude practice usually went, but she definitely felt quite grateful. She was eager to share her discovery with Vera.

She had already made plans to visit Vera tomorrow, on Christmas Eve, to deliver her gift. She would tell her then.

## *Chapter* Twenty-Nine

THE SHOPS IN the Valley of Artisans were all open on Christmas Eve, and River Carter's Pottery Works was no exception.

All day, River was constantly moving—greeting customers, ringing up sales, and carrying stock from the back to the shelves out front. In a rare quiet moment, she boxed Vera's gift—a pitcher from her winter collection—and wrapped it, ready to take to her friend's house that evening.

But River was even more excited about what she had to tell Vera.

After River had realized all she had to be grateful for regarding her health, she had become curious and had done a little more detective work with her calendar. What she had found, she definitely wanted to talk to Vera about.

When the last customer had been helped, the lights turned off, and the doors locked, River loaded Vera's gift into her car and headed for that lady's house, as arranged.

The two planned to have a short visit, over coffee and muffins. River still had preparations to make at her house for her family's Christmas gathering the following day.

As often happens in Indiana, Christmas Eve was warmer than a spring day. Everyone knew the balmy temperature wouldn't stay long, but were definitely enjoying it while it lasted.

Vera welcomed River into her kitchen, where childhood memories of being here with Grandma Ella connected with River's own adult friendship with Vera. It was a gift, River thought, to have a friend who understood so much about the roots of one's life.

Vera loved the pitcher, and that made River happy. Vera presented River with a gift, as well. It was a copy of the third volume of C.S. Lewis's collected letters.

"Oh, Vera!" River exclaimed when she had removed the paper. Vera smiled.

"You were so excited about the second volume when you found it, that I thought you would enjoy this," she said.

"Oh, wow," said River with a smile. "You know I'll *love* it. Thank you."

"And thank you for this beautiful pitcher. I'll make it the centerpiece of my table for the rest of the winter," Vera said, carefully sliding the plate of cranberry muffins toward them and placing the handmade pitcher in the place of honor.

Vera noticed that River's eyes were bright and she seemed unusually animated.

"You look like the cat that swallowed the canary, River. What's going on?"

"Vera, I've realized that ever since you prayed for my healing last summer, the memory issues began getting better—and I mean *better*. When I really started looking into it, I realized I don't even need my workarounds and helps anymore—and I haven't for a while. *And*, I have not had another cognitive glitch. It's been *months*."

Vera watched River's face intently as she talked.

"But what does that really mean?" River asked. "How do I know if it will all stay that way? Just because I haven't had a cognitive glitch in a *while*, couldn't I still *have* another one? I don't know how to know when something that unpredictable is really *gone*."

In the space of the minute it had taken River to say the words, her feelings seemed to have traveled the pendulum from elation to the brink of disappointment.

"From what you've said," Vera began thoughtfully, "it seems apparent that God has done *something*, even if you're not sure yet exactly what it is. So, it seems right to thank him. The fact that you aren't sure what to call it—I understand that. But he will receive glory if you just say what you know is true: that you haven't had a neurocognitive glitch since X date, and that, after needing memory helps for years, you no longer need them."

River looked relieved, and the two were silent for a moment as River considered Vera's words.

"Yes. Okay," said River. "He *definitely* did something."

"He does that," said Vera, matter-of-factly.

River thanked Vera for her advice, and then turned the conversation toward her friend, asking about her writing. Vera shared about some of her research for the new project, which River found fascinating.

"I can't wait to read your book," said River.

"Me, too," laughed Vera. "So, how are things going with your decisions about the sign business?"

"I've been praying for guidance about what to do, but I haven't really heard an answer yet," said River. "Nick's still in town for now, so he's still running the shop over the café 'til he gets a job and leaves."

"He's definitely going?" Vera asked.

"Yeah. It looks like Uncle Jim and Sara are over as a couple."

"That's sad," said Vera.

"Nick said Uncle Jim told him it was because Sara believes in miracles, and Jim doesn't."

Vera was quiet for a while.

Finally, she spoke. "Your grandma, Ella, was taught the same thing when she was young—that miracles didn't happen anymore," said Vera.

Vera would know. She and Ella had been best friends.

"I can remember hearing a story when I was a kid at our church in Tennessee," said River, "of God healing a woman who had advanced cancer. They said her doctor was extremely surprised when she went back for a checkup and she had no cancer. My family didn't know her. I guess it had happened around twenty years before my family even went to that church.

"Things like that—you know, actual *miracles*— do *occasionally* still happen, don't they?" asked River, after a pause. "Maybe you'd hear about it once in a lifetime?"

The humming of the refrigerator rose to fill the silence as she waited for the older woman's response.

"Some people have decided that God *doesn't* do miracles anymore on earth," said Vera. "And then, some think that he *can*, but he *probably won't*, so they don't really expect him to very often."

After a pause, River addressed her friend. "What about you? What do you believe?"

"He *is* doing miracles," Vera said, "and much more often than you've been hearing about."

River felt the weight of truth in Vera's words.

"I know you care about your uncle and about Sara," said Vera. "You could ask God to reveal the truth to Jim."

Later that evening, as River was vacuuming her house in preparation for the next day's festivities, she mentally replayed her conversation with Vera. Sometimes it really seemed as if Vera was seeing something that River couldn't.

*God, let Uncle Jim—and me—see what is true.*

# *Chapter* Thirty

RIVER AWOKE ON Christmas morning to the sound of her brother cooking—and singing—in her kitchen. It was nice to have a culinary expert in charge of the family feast today, even if he didn't quite know all the words to the Christmas song he was belting out as he chopped and stirred.

River quickly showered and dressed, and then checked her phone. Her parents had texted late the night before to say that they'd arrived at The Old Lantern Inn. Since Nick was living in River's guest room, they'd decided to take the opportunity to stay at the newly remodeled B&B. There was a new text from her dad this morning, saying they'd come over after breakfast.

River went to the refrigerator and pulled out some coconut milk kefir and raspberries for her own breakfast.

"You want some of this?" she asked Nick.

"Already ate, but thanks."

"What time did you get up, anyway?" asked River, surveying the extensive preparations already underway in the kitchen.

"Not too much before you." Nick laughed. "I'm just a fast cook."

"I guess so," said River with admiration. It appeared that her brother was pulling out all the stops of his culinary training.

River had finished cleaning the house the night before, but she still needed to iron a tablecloth and set the table. So as soon as she was done with breakfast, she went to get out the ironing board.

She braced her ears for the screeching sound of setting up the ironing board. River thought she might have heard freight trains emergency brake more quietly.

Soon, she had a colorful tablecloth draped over the board. She took satisfaction in watching obstinate wrinkles and creases submit to the heat, steam, and pressure of the iron.

The dining table gradually grew more and more festive, as River filled it with plates, napkins, flatware, and empty serving dishes awaiting Nick's creations. She had gifted herself a complete set of her own winter pottery collection for the occasion, but had mixed in a few of her favorite holiday pieces of Grandma Ella's, as well.

She found herself transported into the flow of creativity as she artfully arranged the pieces on the table.

Her reverie was interrupted by Nick's voice.

"Hey, I think I hear their car," he said over his shoulder, as he stirred something on the stove.

Ted and Andrea Carter came bearing two pumpkin pies from Aunt Della.

"I was afraid if we didn't get them out of there, the other B&B breakfasters at the café would eat them," laughed River's dad.

"Oh, Ted," smiled his wife. "Those pies were all the way back in the kitchen."

The two hugged their children and surveyed the kitchen and dining room.

"I'd say our timing is perfect," said River's dad. "It looks like you two have it all under control."

"Actually, Dad," said River, "you can help me gather up the dining room chairs. They're kind of scattered all over the house."

"How many do we need?" asked her father.

"It's the four of us and Aunt Della and Uncle Jim, so all six of them," said River. "Uncle Jim was going to bring over an extra chair from the café when there were going to be seven of us, but now that Sara's not coming, mine are enough."

"What a sad turn," said River's mom. "I am already missing Sara, and I had just met her."

"I'm sad for them, *and* for me," said Nick.

"Me, too," said River.

"Well, let's not talk about it in front of Jim," said River's dad. "He can bring it up if he wants to, but I don't think we should."

❧❧

Later, when Nick's feast had been thoroughly enjoyed, the family turned their attention to Aunt Della's pies. It would be hard to say how many of her pies they had eaten over the years; they were always a highlight of any gathering.

As Della scooped out each piece and her nephew passed the plates, River spoke up.

"There's some good news I want to share with everyone," she began.

Nick wondered what this might be; he hadn't heard anything about his sister having news, and he'd been living here right under River's nose.

River went on to tell her family about what had happened the previous year—about the pricing mistake that nearly cost her the grand opening of her pottery shop, and why the mistake had happened. She confessed how hard it had been for her to regain her confidence after that, not knowing when something equally problematic might happen again. After all, she had been living proof that time did *not* heal all.

She then recounted that Vera had prayed for her healing several months ago, but that it had been only recently—days ago, in fact—that River had realized she'd experienced no neurocognitive glitches since then.

"And even the daily memory stuff has improved," said River, excitedly. "I realized that I've stopped needing to rely on all of the helps and workarounds that my brain needed for years."

Her smile told her family how she felt about these health gains.

"This is amazing," said Ted Carter, putting his arm around his wife. He and every person around that table could remember when River had lost her balance and manual dexterity, and so much else. Before moving here last year, River had already recovered so much of the neurocognitive function that toxic mold exposure had taken from her. He and Andrea had thought then that their daughter might be as recovered as she would ever be. So, *this* news—this was unexpected.

"Oh, River, we're so happy for you," said her mother, face alight.

"That's awesome, Riv!" Nick chimed in.

Aunt Della was quiet. She had watched something cross Jim's face as he had listened intently to River recount her experience. What had it been? Astonishment? The very earliest glimmer of hope? Her eyes remained fixed on her brother.

"Is there some medical test that could confirm all of this scientifically?" asked Uncle Jim, without giving a hint of what he was feeling.

In the midst of the celebratory atmosphere, the question caught River off-guard, but her father replied.

"Well, there's a specialized brain scan that her doctor in Louisville does. It images environmental toxins in the brain and can show some of their effects on the brain," said Ted. "But it's pretty pricey—in the thousands," he added.

Her great-uncle turned to River. "I'll pay for it," he said. "Can you have one done?"

Everyone around the table knew that this wasn't a good time for a store owner to be away from her business. Many tourists who had come to the Valley for a holiday getaway—and others who would drive there just for a day—would be shopping in full force beginning tomorrow, the day after Christmas.

But River and everyone else around the table realized what Jim was really asking for.

"Of course," she answered immediately. "I'll call tomorrow morning as soon as they open and see how soon I can get an appointment."

## *Chapter* Thirty-One

RIVER WAS ALONE at her house the next morning when she made the call to the medical clinic. Her parents had driven back home to Tennessee last night; her mother's store would have a busy retail day today, being the day after Christmas. River herself was ready to walk out the door to open her own shop for what she hoped would be a banner sales day. And Nick had left for the café hours ago to help Della with the early morning baking.

The moment River had hung up, she called Uncle Jim.

"They just had an opening on Monday due to a cancellation, so I scheduled it," River told him.

Jim thanked his great-niece and asked if she would let him drive her to the appointment. "I'd like to be there," he said.

"Sure, Uncle Jim," River replied. "It would be nice to have your company."

"Hold on a second," said Jim. River heard indistinct conversation between Jim and Della, followed by some shuffling noises in her ear, and then Nick's muffled voice.

Jim came back on. "Della says she can spare both us men on Monday since she only has the B&B breakfast group to feed that day. And Nick says he will cover the pottery shop for you all day Monday," said Uncle Jim.

River knew that Della and Nick would have done much more than that to help Jim. As would they all.

## *Chapter* Thirty-Two

ON MONDAY, RIVER met Uncle Jim at the café and they headed out to get things looked at from another perspective.

After River entered the room with the imaging machine, her doctor administered the imaging dye and then River got onto the table that gently conveyed her under the scanner.

She answered a series of questions, while the machine quietly beeped and recorded images of the inner structures of her brain at work.

The phrase "a penny for your thoughts" came to mind, as River thought of all the money Uncle Jim was spending on this test.

When the imaging was complete, the doctor invited River to sit on a black rolling chair in front of a computer station. The doctor sat down next to her and pulled up River's previous scan on the screen, side-by-side with today's scan.

"Alright. Let's compare today's scan with your last one," she said.

Something told River to ask if her uncle could come in to hear the report, so she made the request.

"Sure," said her doctor.

River stepped out to the hall to speak to Jim, who followed her back into the room. He stood behind her as she sat down again next to the doctor, who seemed engrossed in the images before her.

"Actually," said the doctor, "I'd like to repeat the new scan before we discuss it. Could you both wait here for a moment?" She briskly left the room.

When the doctor returned a few minutes later, another doctor was with her, whom she cursorily introduced by name as a colleague.

"Could you please lie down in the imaging pod again?" asked River's doctor.

As Uncle Jim and the second doctor silently stood by, River's doctor repeated the test. River again heard the soft beep-beep-beep of the machine taking another set of images.

"Okay, you can sit up now," her doctor said to River. "Give us a moment to review these and then I'll have you both sit down in front of the screens."

The two doctors huddled in front of the screens. From behind them, River could see that there were now three sets of images on the screen. Two had today's date but different time stamps, and both looked exactly alike to River. The third was an earlier scan from just a few years ago, when her mold-toxin-injured brain had struggled mightily with everything it had been called upon to do, including cognition, memory, balance, and fine motor skills.

The two doctors talked quietly between themselves as they stared at the screens. River noticed a look of incredulity on her doctor's face, as the woman studied the colorful images of the inside of River's brain.

"I can't explain it either," the colleague said to River's doctor, "but I am seeing what you're seeing. There is no evidence of either toxins or damage."

*No evidence?* thought River. *How was that possible?*

"Well, River," said her doctor, slowly rotating in the swivel chair to face her and Uncle Jim. "I just wanted to get a second set of medical eyes on this. If I hadn't done this imaging myself and I wasn't sitting here looking at these images of your brain in real time, I'd think this was a mistake and that I was looking at someone else's brain on these screens. What we are seeing is an exceptional occurrence."

The other doctor nodded in agreement.

"Why don't you both come sit here," said River's doctor, gesturing to River and Jim as she and the other doctor stood up. River and her great-uncle obeyed.

"I've never seen this before," said the doctor, standing to one side, "and I can't explain it. What the new images from today show," she said, pointing here and there on the screens without touching them with the non-business-end of her pen, "is absolutely no evidence of toxins, or any of their effects on the brain. Which, in your situation, is not just unusual, but medically speaking, is not possible."

As River tried to accept the enormity of what the woman was saying, her uncle, who had had a front-row seat to River's life since she was born and who knew her story, spoke up for the first time in that room.

"You mean, it's a miracle," said Jim.

"By definition of that word," said the doctor, "yes."

As they stepped out of the elevator, Jim called Sara to ask if he could come see her the minute he was back in town.

Before his car departed the medical building parking lot, the entire family heard River's good news from Uncle Jim—who, with her okay, called each one to tell them he had seen the evidence of a miracle.

So, River thought. Her own healing had become the living proof to Uncle Jim that God still does miracles.

She silently thanked God for showing them both the truth in such a clear way.

River had left her car at the café that morning, so when they arrived back in town in the early evening, Uncle Jim dropped her off at the café and he went directly on to the gallery.

River had already called Kate and Vera during the drive back, but she felt like celebrating her good news.

Aunt Della wasn't home, so River let herself into the café entrance using her key. She went upstairs to Signs and Wonders to buy a sign from her own company.

Downstairs, she laid the money for her purchase on the counter with a scribbled note to Nick, asking him to ring up the sale.

It was nearly closing time at the pottery shop, where Nick would be locking up for her any minute. River decided to go by Vera's house to talk to her friend in person before heading home.

"The thing is," River told Vera, "this *is* amazing to me, but it also seems like just the most normal thing—like *this* is how life is supposed to be."

"I think the reason for that," said Vera, "is that both of those things are true."

❧❧

By the time River's head was on the pillow that night, the lives of her family had changed.

Jim and Sara had phoned. The wedding was back on, for New Year's Day—and not by any "agree to disagree" arrangement. The couple was now in harmony. River's healing had shown Uncle Jim that Jesus hadn't flipped the *Open for Miracles* sign around to *Closed for Season*.

Aunt Della had called to say everyone was invited to her house for a pre-wedding dinner on New Year's Eve.

River had talked to her parents, who were thrilled with all of the news, and said they planned to arrive in the Valley in time for Della's New Year's Eve dinner, and would be staying at the B&B until after the wedding.

And when Nick got home to River's that night, he was bursting with happiness—both for River, and because his plans to come to the Valley to live and help run the café were back on, which, he noted, also meant the Signs and Wonders store over the café could remain open.

# *Chapter* Thirty-Three

THE NEXT MORNING, Sara called her friend Marian at the wedding chapel to tell her the wedding was back on.

"I realize that January 1 is just two days away," Sara began, after a friendly greeting, "but I was wondering if, by chance, you kept our chapel reservation on the books as you mentioned?"

Marian was thrilled for the couple, and congratulated her friend profusely.

"I did keep your reservation on the books, Sara, but I'm afraid the chapel still has no electricity at all. That part the electrician needs still hasn't arrived, so the chapel is cold and dark."

If it were just a matter of lighting, Marian explained, she might venture to suggest candles for illumination, but they all knew how cold it was when they had visited before. It was even colder now, and with temperatures predicted to fall further later in the week, there was simply no way it could be done.

"Even if we brought in space heaters powered by a gas generator, it would still be like having an outdoor wedding in Antarctica," Marian lamented emphatically.

"Is there any chance at all that the electrical work could still be finished in time?" Sara asked.

An uncharacteristic sigh came through the receiver from Marian's end.

"I don't see how," Marian admitted. "I was told that the part that was supposed to be in *weeks ago* was on a ship that was caught in a storm. A large number of cargo containers went overboard, and, apparently, the part I need is at the bottom of an ocean somewhere. A replacement will be shipped, of course, if it hasn't already been, but the electrician says there's no way it will arrive in time. They are still trying everything they can think of, but it is not looking good."

"Oh," said Sara, feeling somewhat deflated. "What in the world *is* it?"

"I really don't know," Marian confessed. "Some made-up sounding thing with a bunch of letters and numbers in its name that I wouldn't recognize if it bit me. My expertise is in organizing beautiful events—definitely not in construction.

"But *obviously*," she added sadly, "I am *so* sorry about this. I had really looked forward to having your and Jim's wedding at the chapel."

Marian promised to let Sara know if anything changed.

Well, *this* was a wrinkle in their wedding plans, thought Sara. But at least there was going to *be* a wedding. Sara was disappointed about losing the beauty of the chapel for their special occasion, but she refused to lose her joy over the fact that there was now going to *be* a marriage, when just 24 hours ago, that hadn't been the case.

She called Jim. Together, the pair wondered whether they should try to find a new location on two-days' notice, or perhaps delay the wedding until the chapel could be ready, since they really did want the wedding to be there.

Their hearts had been set on January 1, and then broken when the wedding had been called off. Wouldn't the best way to celebrate their newfound victory be to keep the original wedding date they had chosen? *Yes*, they both agreed. January 1 would be the happy day.

They had already re-invited their friends and family to witness their vows. Now all they needed was a place to *make* those vows—in only two days' time.

## *Chapter* Thirty-Four

AT LUNCH TIME that day, River stopped by Sara's house to present her special wedding gift to Sara and Uncle Jim as they had arranged that morning.

Sara had said they were planning to move Jim's desk from the guest house to his new office at Sara's house over the lunch hour, so that would be a good time to catch them both.

When River arrived, she saw Uncle Jim's empty work truck in the driveway, its tailgate down. Sara's open garage door revealed several pieces of furniture, plus stacks of boxes of the relics of living—some coming, and some going.

"Hello!" River called into the open door between the garage and the house. "It's River!"

"Come on back here!" Sara called from a room at the end of the hallway.

Uncle Jim's desk was now ensconced in the room, and it appeared he was, too. He sat in his old wooden swivel desk chair and beamed at River as she entered the room.

Sara gave River a hug and told her how thrilled she was for her. Sara's eyes glistened as Jim interjected, repeating the words of River's doctor, "by the very definition of the word *miracle*, this is one."

"And I'm thrilled for *you two*," River returned.

"Thank you," said Sara, as her fiancé beamed.

Sara explained about the issue with the wedding chapel, and said they were trying to figure out a plan. "It's still going to be January first, but now we just have to figure out *where*."

"Well, wherever it ends up being, I can't wait to be there," said River.

She presented her wedding gift to the couple: a complete set of her new line of winter dinnerware, featuring snowy scenes with a border of evergreen trees and red ribbons. Uncle Jim and Sara loved the pottery, and thanked her, with hugs and smiles.

"Well, I need to run," said River. "I'll see you tomorrow night!"

As they heard River's car backing out of the driveway, Sara carried one of the plates from River's handmade set to the dining room, where the china cabinet sat, full, and surrounded by boxes. "These dishes River made are absolutely gorgeous. I love them, and I can't wait to use them. Now, what can we get rid of to make room for them?"

# *Chapter* Thirty-Five

As SHE DROVE the short distance back to River Carter's Pottery Works, River pondered the miracle of her own healing, and how one miracle could change the lives of so many people. How it already *had*.

It was also changing *her* expectation about God and her view of his identity and his activity. If he was willing to do this, she wondered, what else was he up to, in general? Was his agenda different than she had thought?

And did it follow, then, that the purpose of her own life could be very different than she had understood it to be? Instead of rushing full steam ahead into anything she *could* do, should she be more purposeful about discovering what she *should* do?

Should she allow her life to be deep enough in one direction for life to flow strongly there, like a river, rather than dissipate her focus until she was a shallow creek bed?

Just then, River had a new experience. She didn't hear a voice, or see anything unusual. But in the space of a few seconds or less, she received an understanding of something she hadn't previously had. That understanding had a significant weight to it, such that she innately understood that it was from God.

River didn't have a word for what had just happened; she had never had this experience before, nor heard anyone she knew describe it. But God had suddenly revealed to her that his idea for her life was different than she had previously imagined—and that, going forward, the Signs and Wonders business was not part of it.

River didn't know exactly what God's idea for her life *was*—but she felt excited about it— energized.

And she realized that her prayer for him to direct her paths about the sign shop had been answered. She didn't have a detailed map of her whole life, but she definitely had her answer about whether to follow that particular trail.

Now she just had to figure out what to do about it.

## *Chapter* Thirty-Six

THE HOURS WERE slipping by. It was already Tuesday afternoon, and the proposed wedding—the one without a chapel—was to be on Thursday.

Sara had returned to her gallery after lunch, and Jim to the guest house to finish packing for his move. They knew they had to make a decision—and soon. If the chapel wasn't going to be ready, where else could they even have the wedding?

Sara's entire house was a renewed hub of boxes and belongings coming and going—they both agreed that no one could get married *there* in two-day's time. Jim's house, while attractive, didn't have a room spacious enough to hold the number of friends they had invited. His living room, like River's, was nicely sized for holding a family gathering—but not a wedding. And the café—while available and large enough—didn't seem nearly as romantic to either of them as the chapel.

But at this point, it was really too late to find anywhere else for a January 1 wedding. It wasn't as if any of the area's church buildings, the Community Center, or anywhere else could even be reserved on such short notice—especially on a holiday, when such venues would be certain to have other events already planned. Sara and Jim had already called every place they could think of and had been told as much.

As the couple ran down their phone batteries throughout the afternoon, comparing notes as the minutes and hours passed, they reluctantly came to the conclusion that the wedding would just have to be at the café.

Late that afternoon, Sara called Marian to see if there had been any change in the situation at the chapel.

"I'm sorry, Sara," said Marian, "but it's still dark and cold."

"We understand," said Sara, "I just wanted to check. We really want to go ahead with a January 1 wedding, so it looks like it will need to be at the café."

Marian, in an effusion of apology about the chapel, offered to bring wedding decorations to prepare the café on the morning of January 1. Sara gladly accepted Marians' offer. *She* certainly didn't have time to do anything about decorations.

As the two friends said their goodbyes, Sara suddenly realized that she and Jim didn't have a marriage license yet. Was tomorrow a government holiday? She didn't know, but she knew she didn't want *anything else* to get in the way of this wedding.

Sara grabbed her bag and ran to the front of the gallery. Thankfully, there were no customers just then. She hastily dialed Jim as she turned the sign to *Closed* and locked the front door, trying not to drop her phone as she did.

"Marriage license! Courthouse! Meet me there! I'm leaving now!"

## *Chapter* Thirty-Seven

RIVER HAD JUST gotten home that evening and was hopefully exploring the contents of her refrigerator to see what might be for dinner, when Sara called.

"The wedding is being moved to the café," Sara said, "because the chapel doesn't have lights or heat yet—there's some electrical issue."

"I'm sorry to hear that about the chapel," said River. "I know how much you wanted the ceremony to be there."

Sara thanked River, and was philosophical about the chapel situation, saying it couldn't be helped. "We're just happy there's going to be a wedding," she told River, with a smile in her voice.

Sara said she couldn't talk long, that she still needed to call more people, but that she would see River tomorrow at Della's dinner.

As River returned to foraging for her own dinner, she thought back to Thanksgiving and

Sara's exuberance at the idea of her later-in-life marriage. What a mountain of heartache Sara and Uncle Jim had recently crossed to even *get* to this point, with their wedding now less than two days away. River thought of how happy it would make both of them to be able to have their ceremony in the beautiful chapel.

She wondered whether this would be an appropriate matter to ask God to intervene in. Healing was one thing, but did God really concern himself with pulling out all the stops for less weighty matters? Was it selfish to ask him to do something about the lights and heat in a tiny wedding chapel in Indiana?

Vera had said River should tell God what she needed. Did this qualify as a *need?* Or was it just a want? Did God spend his energy and time on *wants?* Was it even right to ask him to? Should she ask Vera about this?

River decided that instead of asking herself these questions, or asking Vera, she would just ask God, the way a child would. *God, please do something so that Sara and Jim can get married at the wedding chapel on Thursday.*

After she had finished eating dinner, River sat at the table, quietly letting her thoughts catch up with her. She'd been so busy all afternoon with customers that she hadn't had time to consider her response to the revelation she'd received at lunchtime about the direction of her own life.

Now, as she replayed the experience in her mind, she knew what to do.

She reached for her phone and sent a text to her brother, who was still at the café: *Can we talk when you get home tonight?*

## *Chapter* Thirty-Eight

THANKFULLY, NICK WASN'T too late getting home.

Since the café would only be open for breakfast tomorrow, kitchen prep had been light.

"So, what's up?" he said, flopping onto the couch in the family room. River was already sitting in the chair, where her hummingbird pillow had given way for the season to a pillow bearing the script COME, LET US WORSHIP.

"Nick, I really liked the idea of the sign business. *Obviously*—I'm the one who started it. And I'm extremely grateful to know that I have the physical *capacity* for it."

Nick sat up and leaned toward his sister, intently watching her face. This didn't sound like anything he'd been expecting to hear, although he wasn't sure *what* he'd been expecting when River had asked for this talk.

"But I know something now that I didn't know before. That capacity is intended for something different than what I've been using it for."

River told her brother about her experience in the car that day at lunchtime—about the revelation she had received about her life. "It answered the question for me about my role in the Signs and Wonders business," said River.

"I still have more to figure out, but I know now that I'm going to focus most of my time and energy on pottery, and I'm going to be very intentional about what else I add to my life."

"I've realized that, while there's nothing wrong with taking a fun vacation—and I'm not saying I still won't go on one—I want a kind of life that I don't *need* to take a vacation from in order to survive. And my life was starting to feel that way— even though I really liked the idea of the sign business at the beginning."

Nick continued to listen, but had leaned back on the couch, resting a hand on each knee.

"The thing is," River went on, "even though I know I need to get completely out of the sign business, I'm not quite sure how to extricate myself from it now. I don't want to let down my business partners, since I'm the one who started it and kind of drew them all on board. Kate, Danny, Sara—they're all *friends*."

River faltered. She picked up the decorative pillow that rested beside her and, crossing her arms over it, clutched it to herself, gripping its outer edges with both hands.

"I think I may have a solution for you," said Nick, a smile beginning to develop at one corner of his mouth. "I'd be interested in taking over for you with Signs and Wonders."

"Oh, no, Nick, you don't have to do—," River began.

But Nick held up a hand. "Hear me out," he invited. "I really enjoy the business, and I would appreciate having a second income stream from something like that that dovetails so well with my work at the café.

"I want to save money so I can be prepared to buy out the café one day when Jim and Della are ready to retire. I expect that's still a long way off— which is a good thing, for all of us. Anyway, Della says her sons won't want the café, and neither Jim nor Sara has any kids *to* want it.

"So, if you and your business partners agree, I'd like to take over your role and your share in Signs and Wonders."

This was the first time River had heard her brother speak of such long-range plans for putting down deep roots in the Valley of Artisans. He seemed to already have a vision for his life. She unfurled her arms from the pillow and let it rest loosely on her lap, where she stacked her hands on top of it.

"Alright, then," said River. "I'll talk to the others and give you an answer."

"You know," said Nick, "maybe you did nothing wrong in *starting* the business—maybe God was preparing it to be ready for *me* the whole time."

River raised her eyebrows thoughtfully. "Maybe. I'm sure I don't know. I really don't think about it in terms of right and wrong, though," she added, and then paused. "But I can tell you one thing. I'm going to go about things differently from now on."

She didn't know how to put into words—even to such a trusted confidante as her brother—that she had realized while she might be the sculptor of her own life, the *greatest* possibilities for that life would come from *sharing* that creative endeavor with the one who had sculpted *her*. And *that* was something she was quite eager to do.

## *Chapter* Thirty-Nine

WHEN MARIAN RYAN, owner of the wedding chapel, opened the front door of her house to leave early on the morning of New Year's Eve, she was greeted by a blast of cold air, a high-pitched bark from the tiny dog who guarded the entry door sidelights in the house across the street, and a plastic bag sitting on her welcome mat. Only two of those things had been expected.

She stooped gingerly to look into the plastic bag with one free hand, careful not to tip her lidded coffee mug or spill her heavy purse from her shoulder, but she didn't recognize the bag's contents. Marian wondered what it was and how it had gotten there, but no explanation seemed to be forthcoming.

Ever punctual, she didn't permit the mystery to delay her. She picked up the bag, adding it to her burden, and proceeded to her car, which had been warming up in the driveway. Maybe one of the contractors would know something about it.

When Marian arrived at the chapel to retrieve the decorations she'd need for the January 1 wedding at the café, she took the bag inside with her.

"Yoo-hoo," she called as she entered, over the noise of the gas generators just outside the side door. Although there had been one work truck out front, she didn't see anyone around. In fact, other than the generators themselves, which were now running just enough heaters to keep the plumbing from freezing, there didn't seem to be much evidence of work in progress. Instead, the chapel appeared to be completed. Marian stood at the top of the aisle, taking it all in. The place had been in such disarray for so long during the restoration, that the order and unobstructed beauty took her aback.

"Miz Ryan?" called a man in a brown coverall, peeking in from an open side door, and blinking as his eyes adjusted from the brightness outside. "Well, it is you. I thought I heard someone in here. I just came to refill the generators."

It was Chuck, the electrician.

"Good morning, Chuck," Marian replied. "I wanted to see if you know anything about *this.*" She held out the plastic bag.

Chuck briskly closed the distance between them, and peered inside the bag.

"Where did you get this?" he asked, eyeing Marian's face.

She told him the story of finding the bag outside her front door that morning. "Why? Do you know something about it?" she asked.

"It's the part we need to finish the job," said the electrician.

"It's the *what?*" exclaimed Marian. "But why would—"

"Here, hand me that part," Chuck interjected, "and let's get this project finished. You'll have heat and lights in here in about an hour."

Fifty-six minutes later, Sara's phone rang. It was Marian. One minute after that, Jim's phone rang. It was Sara. The heat and lights were on. The wedding would be at the chapel.

His work at the wedding chapel completed, Chuck returned to his shop. He had a phone call of his own to make, to his supplier, about this bizarre part delivery. Of all the unprofessional nonsense he'd seen in his day, this ranked right up there near the top, and he wanted some answers.

"Why didn't that part come to my business?" demanded Chuck into speaker phone. "It was delivered to my *client's* house—Marian Ryan—left on the front porch, *out* of its box, and it *wasn't even marked!*"

But the supplier had no idea what Chuck was talking about.

"Sir, our system shows that the part you ordered hasn't arrived in the U.S. yet. And we have no record or address for anyone named Marian Ryan."

## *Chapter* Forty

THE MORNING OF New Year's Eve was a busy one at River Carter's Pottery Works. River was glad to see so many shoppers; these holiday visitors to the Valley were good for business, hers included.

As she smiled and chatted with people, River noticed herself regarding her customers as *part* of her business, rather than as an interruption to her production schedule, as she realized she had begun to. She was enjoying interacting with them. It made her feel deeply peaceful, somehow, to not be thinking there was something else she should— or could—be doing, other than exactly what she *was* doing.

Traffic dropped off sharply in the late afternoon, and River decided to close her shop an hour early. There was something she needed to take care of. After a quick phone call to Kate, River stowed her lunch bag in her car, before running down the sidewalk in the frigid air to the woodworking shop. The crowds at Danny and Kate's woodworking shop had also dwindled to nothing in the cold early evening, after a successful day.

The three conferenced in Sara by phone for the shortest owners' meeting the Signs and Wonders proprietors had ever held. River explained to Kate and Danny and Sara why she wanted to transfer her place in that business to her brother. Her partners—her friends—understood. They said they'd be happy to welcome Nick into that role— he'd instantly gelled well with the group from the first time they'd met together.

"All right. It's settled then," said River, with satisfaction. "I'm out. Nick is in. Meeting adjourned. Thank you, all."

After Sara hung up, Danny gave River a soft clap on the back with one dry, cracked carpenter's hand.

"I don't know why I'm congratulating you on leaving a growing business that you started," he said, with a lopsided smile, "but somehow it just seems right."

"It's been an incredible week," said Kate, giving her friend a hug. "I'm very happy for you."

"Thanks, guys," said River, returning their genuine smiles. "I'm happy for me, too."

The decision had been finalized. River was handing her part in Signs and Wonders to Nick.

River set out for the short walk to her car. Bitterly cold air fell through the fabric of her thick jeans as if it were on a mission to commit frostbite, and she was grateful for silk long underwear. She composed a text message to her brother as she walked: *Partners have all agreed. I'm out, you're in. Congrats! See you tonight.*

As she sat in her car waiting for the cold engine to warm up for the short drive home to change for dinner, River called Vera.

River told her friend about deciding to pray for the chapel to be ready in time for the wedding tomorrow, and then, somehow—she didn't know how—it was.

She told Vera about the revelation she'd received for her own life, and how she knew she had to leave the sign business behind—and then how Nick had surprised her by wanting to step in.

Vera listened to all of River's news, expressing her gladness for the family over the development with the chapel, and commending River for her responsiveness to the leading she'd received.

"Even when everything still isn't clear to you," said Vera, "you've aligned yourself with what you heard."

"You know, Nick said something yesterday about not thinking it was wrong for me to start the sign business," said River. "But I told him I didn't really see it in those terms."

"I would agree with you there," said Vera. "Maybe it's more like... tuning an instrument."

"That makes sense."

"Except it takes a lifetime," said Vera, with a happy laugh that somehow reminded River of birdsong.

The two wished each other Happy New Year, and River headed home.

## *Chapter* Forty-One

IN HER DRIVEWAY, River turned off the car and began to gather her things from the front seat. As she did, she saw the sign she had bought on Monday, still on the passenger floorboard where she had put it. She picked it up to bring inside.

River had no more than stepped inside when she was surprised to hear Nick's car. A moment later, he ran in the back door.

"Hey, Riv!" he greeted his sister.

"Hey, I didn't expect to see you here before dinner," said River, depositing her lunch bag on the counter and then her leather bag onto a kitchen chair.

"I didn't expect to *be* seen here," Nick replied, "until I looked down at my clothes after the dinner prep and saw what a mess I had made."

"Oh," said River, assessing the damage he referred to. Something that looked like pie filling appeared to have attacked him. "Well, soon, you won't have far to go to change," she said. "But I will miss having you stay here."

"It's been nice," said Nick. "Thanks for letting me crash with you. I think while Dad is in town, I'll ask him to help me move my boxes and things from here over to Jim's guest house after the wedding festivities are over tomorrow."

"Okay, if that's what you want to do," said River, "but there's no hurry, as far as I'm concerned. You're welcome here as long as you like."

"Thanks," Nick smiled.

"What's that?" he asked, gesturing to the sign still in River's hand.

"It's the sign I bought the other night that I left you the note and money on the counter for. It's definitely time to hang it up. Come on, you can help me."

River pulled a hammer and a nail from her kitchen junk drawer.

Nick followed his sister out the front door onto the porch, where she drove a nail and hung the sign with satisfaction.

"*Open for Miracles,*" Nick read. "That sign sure has stories to tell in *this* family."

"You know," confessed River, "when we first came up with that sign design, I really didn't think of it as much more than a clever little saying. But after everything that has happened here in such a short time, I really don't even *know* what might be next. I feel like I really *am* open for miracles."

## *Chapter* Forty-Two

AFTER HUGS AND greetings as they gathered, River's family took their places around Aunt Della's table once again to celebrate. River, Nick, Ted and Andrea, Aunt Della, and Uncle Jim and Sara all chattered excitedly about the wedding tomorrow.

River noticed with pleasure that the table was set with winter dishes she had created.

"So, is this a wedding dinner, or a New Year's Eve party?" Jim teased his sister, Della.

"Yes," she laughed. As much as Della had struggled at first with the realities of letting her brother go from the place he had filled for so long, she had hurt even more at his pain during the breakup with Sara that had nearly kept him from leaving. She knew that Jim and Sara belonged together. And she was immensely happy for them both that now they would be.

Ted spoke up. "I know the last few weeks have been pretty boring for everyone here—" He was interrupted by laughter. "But maybe something exciting will happen next year."

"Oh, I have no doubt that it will," said his aunt.

Della went on to say that she was looking forward to working with Nick, who had turned what she thought would be a very difficult time for her, into a new adventure.

"What is everyone else looking forward to?" asked Della.

"I'm having fun working with you, Aunt Della," said Nick, "and I look forward to continuing to learn from you at the café. *And*—" here Nick's eyes took on the sparkle of one with a happy secret to tell, "as of this afternoon, I'm also a managing partner of Signs and Wonders, which I hope will continue to grow and be the trusty side business it was always intended to be." Nick and River exchanged smiles.

Now it was Ted and Andrea's turn to be surprised, since this was the first they'd heard of that change. Ted shook his head with a smile, and he and everyone else congratulated Nick.

"I think I speak for both of us," said Andrea, with a happy look at her husband, "when I say we are looking forward to continuing to see our children's lives unfold."

Uncle Jim said that after the events of the past month, he wouldn't even know where to start. "But whatever the new year holds," he said, "I look forward to entering the future with my beloved Sara."

"Absolutely," said Sara. "The first thing I am looking forward to in the New Year is our chapel wedding, which, just a month ago, seemed like a somewhat *ordinary* thing, but now—after all that has transpired—is really quite *extra*ordinary."

Everyone agreed.

"River, what about you?" Sara asked.

"I'm looking forward to approaching my life in a new way," said River. "It's kind of hard to explain, but a few weeks ago, I felt like life was some kind of thing involving a boat and wind and waves—and me hanging on while I pressed forward. But it's different now. I think I've just begun to see for the first time *why* Peter got *out* of the boat."

River smiled. "And *that* makes me excited about *whatever* is ahead."

# Visit the Valley of Artisans Again

There is more just waiting for you in the Valley of Artisans series!

### Remembering - Book 1
River Carter arrives in the Valley of Artisans to reopen her family's pottery shop in time for the fall tourist season. But instead of an exciting new beginning, will pain from her past shatter her peace?

### A Winter Wedding in the Valley of Artisans - Book 3
The Valley's charming wedding chapel is finally ready for its grand opening. But when an ice storm brings an unexpected wedding guest with questions for River Carter, where will his inquiries lead?

### Ordinary Miracles - Book 4
River Carter is unexpectedly faced with a challenge to her very beliefs about how God works. As she transforms her neglected garden into a place of inspiring beauty, will she find herself coming to life in a new way, as well?

## Note from the Author

You're invited to join my email community, at https://amylu-riley.com.

Made in the USA
Monee, IL
02 December 2021

83028080R00142